NEVER THE TIME
AND THE PLACE

BY

BETTY

KU-580-310

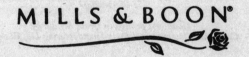

MILLS & BOON®

*MILLS & BOON and MILLS & BOON with the Rose Device
are registered trademarks of the publisher.*

*First published in Great Britain 1985 by Mills & Boon Limited
This edition 1998
Harlequin Mills & Boon Limited,
Eton House, 18-24 Paradise Road, Richmond, Surrey TW9 1SR*

© Betty Neels 1985

ISBN 0 263 81164 6

*Set in Times Roman 10 on 12 pt by
Rowland Phototypesetting Limited
Bury St Edmunds, Suffolk*

73-9803-52009

*Made and printed in Great Britain by
Caledonian International Book Manufacturing Ltd, Glasgow*

Dear Reader,

Looking back over the years, I find it hard to realise that twenty-six of them have gone by since I wrote my first book—*Sister Peters in Amsterdam*. It wasn't until I started writing about her that I found that once I had started writing, nothing was going to make me stop—and at that time I had no intention of sending it to a publisher. It was my daughter who urged me to try my luck.

I shall never forget the thrill of having my first book accepted. A thrill I still get each time a new story is accepted. Writing to me is such a pleasure, and seeing a story unfolding on my old typewriter is like watching a film and wondering how it will end. Happily of course.

To have so many of my books re-published is such a delightful thing to happen and I can only hope that those who read them will share my pleasure in seeing them on the bookshelves again. . .and enjoy reading them.

Betty Neels

Back by Popular Demand

A collector's edition of favourite titles from one of the world's best-loved romance authors. Mills & Boon are proud to bring back these sought after titles and present them as one cherished collection.

BETTY NEELS: COLLECTOR'S EDITION

CHAPTER ONE

THE rain pouring down from a grey, sodden sky, had turned the gold and red of the October afternoon into a landscape of gloom, with rivulets of water trickling on to the road from the high banks on either side of it and a never ending shower of leaves drifting down from the trees clustered behind them. But the girl squelching along the lane didn't in the least mind the weather; to be in the country, away from chimney pots and little mean streets of small dismal houses and the never ending noise, was contentment. She was going at a good pace, well wrapped against the weather, tendrils of bright chestnut hair hanging bedraggled around her pretty face, wet from the rain. She was a tall girl and well built and even the wringing mackintosh she wore couldn't disguise her splendid figure.

There was a dog with her; a black labrador, his sleek coat soaked, plodding along beside her with evident enjoyment, tongue lolling, his eyes turned to her face every moment or so, listening to her quiet voice. 'So you see, Cuthbert, you'll not have me to take you for walks; you'll have to make do with Mike or Natalie when they're home. Of course, I'll come home whenever I can but Yorkshire is a long way.' She came to a halt and stared down at the devoted creature. 'I ought to be feeling

5

very happy, but I'm not. Do you suppose it's wedding nerves? I've got the awful feeling that I don't want to get married at all. Oh, Cuthbert. . .' She bent right down and twiddled his wet ears, and he licked her hand gently.

Very few cars came along the lane and what with the noise of the rain and the wind in the trees, she hadn't heard the car coming up the hill behind them; a Bentley, sliding to a dignified halt within a few feet of them. She stood up then, hushed Cuthbert's indignant bark, and went to poke her head through the window by the driver.

'You should have sounded your horn,' she told the man at the wheel severely. 'You could have run us down.'

She found herself looking into two of the coldest blue eyes she had ever seen. His voice was just as cold. 'Young lady, I am not in the habit of running anyone or anything down. Is this a private road?'

'Lord no. It leads to Ridge Giffard from East Giffard and after that there's Tisbury.'

'I am aware of my surroundings. I was wondering why you had the effrontery to criticise my driving on a public road.'

Gently the girl's softly curving mouth rounded into an indignant O and her large grey eyes narrowed. A rat trap of a mouth in a rugged, handsome face; pepper and salt hair, cut short, and a commanding nose; she surveyed them without haste. At length she said kindly, in the tone of voice one might use to humour an ill tempered child. 'You're touchy, aren't you? And a stranger to these parts?' She straightened up: 'Well, don't let me keep you. You say you're aware of your surroundings, so I won't need to tell you that they'll be moving the cows across at Pake's Farm a mile along on the next bend'. She added, 'A pedigree herd, too.'

The man in the car gave a low rumble of laughter although he didn't look amused. 'No, you don't need to tell me, young lady, but I can see that it gives you a good deal of satisfaction to do so.' He asked to surprise her. 'Are you married?'

And when she shook her head. 'Something for a man to be thankful for.'

She wasn't in the least put out. 'That could be a compliment,' she told him sweetly. 'Mind how you go.'

The cold eyes swept over her before he drove away. It was like a bucket of cold water.

'Anyone else would have offered us a lift,' she told Cuthbert. 'Not that we would have accepted.'

She started walking again, the afternoon would soon turn into an early evening and they had another mile or so to go.

The pair of them negotiated a gate presently and took to the fields, going at a right angle to the road, to cross a stile at the end of the second field and come into a narrow lane running between trees. It went quite steeply down hill in a series of bends, passing a cottage or two on the way until the village appeared; a cluster of cottages, a shop or two and half a dozen larger houses, with ancient tiled roofs and eighteenth century fronts. The girl went past them all, waving once or twice to the few people in the street, and turned in through an open gateway at the end of the village. The drive was short, leading to an outbuilding used as a garage and then turning to broaden out before the low, sprawling house. It was built of red brick like most of the houses in the village but it had a thatched roof and mullioned windows and a very solid front door, ignored by the girl who turned down the side of the house, went through a tumble-down stone archway and opened a door leading from the garden.

The room she went into was small with a stone flagged floor, probably in earlier days a garden room, but now a repository for a collection of shabby coats and mackintoshes, shapeless caps and hats and an untidy row of footwear of all kinds. She took a towel from a peg on the wall, rubbed Cuthbert dry and then took off her own mac and opened another door leading this time to a short passage which in its turn ended in the kitchen. A large, low ceilinged room with an old-fashioned scrubbed table in its centre, windsor chairs at either end of it, and a wooden dresser taking up most of one wall. There was an Aga Stove and a rag rug spread before it on the brick floor, occupied by a tabby cat who hardly moved as Cuthbert flung himself down with a contented sigh. There were a number of doors leading from the room, one of which was partly open.

'Josephine?' asked a muffled voice from behind it, 'is that you, dear? Where did I put the blackcurrant jam; I thought it was on the top shelf. . .'

The pantry door was pushed open and Mrs

Dowling came into the kitchen. They were very alike, mother and daughter, the one still showing signs of the beauty of the other, both with grey eyes and gentle mouths, although Mrs Dowling's hair was heavily streaked with silver.

'Nice walk?' she asked, forgetting the jam.

'Lovely. I can't think why I work in London, Mother, when I could spend my days here...'

'Well, you won't be there much longer, darling. In another month or two you'll be married to Malcolm and I daresay the Yorkshire Moors are just as beautiful as our bit of the country.'

Josephine cut a slice off the loaf on the table and began to eat it. She said thoughtfully, 'Well, yes, they're beautiful, but they're a long way away.'

'You'll have Malcolm's mother and father,' her mother pointed out.

'So I shall,' Josephine agreed slowly. She had fought a long hard battle with herself over her future mother-in-law; they didn't like each other and never would. Josephine, voicing her doubts to Malcolm, had come up against an easy-going amusement which refused to recognise her difficulties. They would settle down nicely, he had assured her, half laughing, it was because they didn't know each other very well, all that would be changed when they saw each other daily. A prospect which made Josephine shudder; Malcolm was going into his father's practice and was perfectly content to live within a stones throw of his parents house; it was one of the things which worried her, especially if she were to wake in the night and think about it, although in the morning her worries seemed rather silly.

She said, 'The jam—it's on the bottom shelf, right at the back. I'll get it.' She emerged presently from the cupboard and put the pot on the table. 'I met a man while I was out. In a Bentley—I've never seen him before—is there someone staying up at the Manor?'

Mrs Dowling was cutting bread and butter. 'Not that I know of, but the Vicar's wife mentioned someone saying they were staying over at Branton House; she didn't know anything about him, though she'd heard that he was a foreigner.'

'I daresay your father will know.'

But presently, sitting round the fire in the comfortable, shabby drawingroom, she forgot about him. Her father, the local GP, had been at Salisbury Hospital, visiting a patient and an old friend after lunching with colleagues, and the talk was of them and their doings. Presently he got up to take evening surgery. Josephine cleared away the tea things and washed the delicate old china and rubbed up the silver spoons which her Mother had always used each day, and then started to prepare the supper. Tomorrow evening, she thought with a sigh, she would be back in London, sitting in her office writing the report; it would be a busy day—theatre day—the gyny ward was always full but the turnover was brisk and for the most part the patients were very cheerful. She loved her work and she was going to miss it when she married Malcolm. It was only recently that she had had niggling doubts; things that hadn't seemed to matter too much now mattered a great deal; Yorkshire was a far cry from Ridge Giffard and she was essentially a home loving girl. She had always been content, living in the old house, coming home from boarding school and then leaving it to train as a nurse, but even then she had come home on her free days, and now, a Ward Sister and the possessor of a second-hand Mini, she found it easy enough to drive to and fro when she had her free weekends. She would miss Mike and Natalie, she didn't see much of them these days for they were both away from home for a good part of the year, Natalie at school taking her O levels and Mike in his first year at medical school. And the house she and Malcolm were to have—it was small and modern and had what she considered to be a pokey little garden. It worried her that she minded that so much. Surely, if she loved Malcolm, it shouldn't matter?

She fed Cuthbert his supper and Mrs Whisker, the tabby, and fetched the lamb cutlets from the fridge. She liked cooking. Now she set to work cooking cucumber gently in a big pan, egg and breadcrumbing the cutlets and adding them to the cucumber and while they were simmering gently, she put on the potatoes and peeped at the celery braising in the oven. Her father would be hungry; the waiting room had been full and the 'phone had been ringing often enough; by the time he had done his evening rounds it would be eight o'clock or half past. Apple crumble and cream would make a nice afters; she set to work happily.

Putting her pie in the oven presently, she wondered idly about the man in the Bentley; he would be hundreds of miles away by now and would have forgotten her entirely. It surprised her that she felt vague regret about this.

He wasn't hundreds of miles away; he was a bare half dozen, having a drink before dinner with his host and hostess at Branton House, exchanging polite conversation about the weather. During a comfortable pause—for they were old friends and didn't need to keep up an unceasing chat—he remarked idly, 'I met a girl as I was coming here. A strapping creature with a lovely face and enormous grey eyes. She had a labrador with her and they both appeared to be enjoying the weather. She gave me a sound telling off for not sounding my horn. I might add that she and the dog were standing in the centre of the road and seemed to consider it to be theirs.'

His hostess laughed. 'Josephine Dowling— she's a darling; the eldest of our doctor's three children. She's a Ward Sister at St Michael's—I daresay you'll meet her.'

The man's eyes were half closed. 'I look forward to that. But perhaps she won't recognise me. . .'

'Don't be silly, Julius.' His hostess smiled widely. He was a tall man powerfully built and dressed with a quiet elegance; moreover, he had a face which a woman wouldn't forget easily. She had no doubt that when Josephine saw him she would know him at once. A pity she was to be married—she might have taken Julius's mind off his recently broken engagement. . .

Twenty-four hours later, Josephine was sitting exactly as she knew she would be, in her office at the end of the landing outside the ward, with the door open so that she could keep an eye on the comings and goings of the visitors. It had been a very busy day; there had been four cases for theatre and Mr Bull, the surgeon, had been in a fiendish temper for all of them so that the Student Nurses who had accompanied the patients had come back with eyes like saucers and a greatly increased knowledge of rude words. After the last case he had come on to the ward looking like a thunder cloud, dragging behind him a posse of reluctant lesser fry, trying to avoid his eye and terrified that he might shoot questions at them as he went from bed to bed. Josephine, quite used to him, gave him a soothing good afternoon and watched him blow out his moustache, a sure sign that he was put out.

'Fools,' he uttered strongly, 'I have nothing but fools to work for me.' Josephine drew herself up to her splendid height and met his choleric eye. 'Not you, Jo—depend on you, don't I? And why you have to go and marry some young fool of a GP. I don't know. . . How's that last patient? I knew I'd find CA, but I think she'll do.'

Josephine led him across the ward to where the operation cases were sleeping peacefully behind their screens. 'She's doing nicely, sir. She came back from the recovery room an hour ago. I'm glad she's okay—her husband 'phoned—he'll be in presently—not to see her, he just wants to know what's happened.'

Mr Bull might have a nasty temper but he was a kind man as well. 'I'll be in the hospital for another hour, if he comes before then let me know I'll have a word with him.'

Josephine beamed at him. 'How nice of you, he'll be so relieved.' She went to the bed while Mr Bull took a look at his patient and then went in turn to the other three.

'Might as well do a quick round,' he muttered and set off with Josephine keeping pace, her Staff Nurse, Joan Makepeace, trotting behind, closely followed by the students.

There were sixteen patients in the ward and half of that number were sufficiently recovered from their operations to gather, cosily dressing-gowned, in little groups and discuss and enlarge upon their various conditions. They did this cheerfully, their troubles nicely behind them, the prospect of going home in the near future buoying up their spirits.

Mr Bull waited a little impatiently while the nurses hurried these ladies back to sit by their beds, and then spoke a few words to each of them. For some reason which Josephine never quite fathomed, his patients, almost without exception, adored him. He wasn't particularly nice to them, but even when imparting some unpleasant news to them he managed to convey his certainty that he would be able to cope with it and restore them to their homes in perfect health.

But most of his time was taken up with the patients who hadn't reached the happy state of shuffling along to the day room, with these he spent time and trouble, reassuring them, reading up their notes carefully, sometimes asking questions that were pertinent to the apprehensive students behind him. His quick round had taken a good half hour and had left Josephine busier than ever, rearranging her patients once more, sending nurses to a tea they had almost missed, giving the Staff Nurse a hand with the evening medicine round. She sat now, waiting for the last of the visitors to go so that she could do her final round and then finish her report, turning over in her mind Mr Bull's parting shot as he marched out of the ward. 'I'm off to Brussels for a month, Jo, lecturing and marking exam papers, heaven help me. An old friend and colleague will be standing in for me; clever bloke, well known and highly thought of.' He had given a guffaw of delighted laughter. 'Don't let him oust that fellow you are going to marry.'

She had said a little starchily, 'That's not likely, sir. I hope you enjoy your stay in Brussels.' And at the same time she had felt a twinge of excitement and interest.

The night staff, coming on duty, interrupted her thoughts; she dismissed them at once and started reading the report.

This took some time; the four operation cases were gone into with meticulous detail and then the remaining ladies discussed at varying lengths. 'And Mrs Prosser,' finished Josephine, referring to an elderly lady who had given more trouble than the whole ward put together, 'Mr Bull sees no reason why she shouldn't go home in two days time—that'll be Saturday. She's dead set on staying the weekend, though, says there'll be no one at home to look after her. Nobody came to see her this evening, so I couldn't discover if that's true or not, but we do need the bed and she's already been in several days longer than usual.'

She got up to go. 'And Mr Bull tells me he'll be going away for a month. He's got someone coming to do his work, though. Have a good night.'

She picked up the big bag she took on duty with her, filled with the impedimenta needed by a young woman cut off from such things as she might require in the way of make-up, her purse, the letters she hadn't had time to read, and an assortment of pens, her gold watch and a spare pair of tights, and left the ward. The nurses who had been on duty with her had already gone, the landing was silent as she crossed it, went through the wide swing doors at the further end and started down the stone staircase. She was in the more modern part of the hospital, but not as modern as all that; woman's surgical and the gyny ward had been built some thirty years before and attached to the central, early Victorian block, a not very happy union, architecturally speaking. It was even worse on the opposite side, where the hospital had been enlarged only recently. It held the most modern of equipment and boasted colour schemes in the wards and such refinements as a tasteful waiting room for relatives, cloakrooms for the nursing staff and silent swift lifts which never broke down. But strangely, the nurses preferred the Victorian wing, despite the lack of colour schemes, even preferring in many cases to work in the central block, where the medical patients were housed in gloomy wards which no amount of modernising would ever disguise.

Josephine sped down the staircase, poked her head round the swing doors of the ward below her own, and finding Mercy Latimer already gone, went on her way. On the ground floor she crossed the entrance hall and went down a dark passage at its back which ended in a large door with 'Nursing Staff Only' painted on it. She went through this into another passage, very clean and smelling of furniture polish, and started up the stairs at the end. The sisters had bed sitting rooms on the first floor, reached by a swing door on the landing and once through that she could hear the steady murmur of voices coming from the end of the corridor before her. She unlocked her door, flung her cap and bag on the bed and went on towards the sound of rattling tea cups.

There were half a dozen young women crammed into the small kitchen, intent on making tea. She was on good terms with them all, for they had all trained, just as she had, at St Michael's.

'Late off, aren't you?' asked Mercy.

'Mr Bull did a round and it took me the rest of the afternoon and evening to catch up. He's going away for a month. . .'

'Bully for you,' the small fair-haired girl

spoke. 'Think of all the empty beds.'

'You'll be lucky.' Caroline Webster, the Senior Theatre Sister, spooned tea into a giant pot. 'There's someone coming to do his work for him. A glutton for work, so I'm told. Coming into theatre tomorrow afternoon with Mr Bull to cast an eye around. I expect you'll get him too, Jo.'

Jo put milk in a mug and spooned in sugar lavishly. 'I hope not, you know what it's like the day after ops, one long rush with drips and dope and the poor dears not feeling their best. And Mrs Prosser,' she added gloomily, 'he'll be someone new to complain to. You see, just as we've got her all fixed up to go home on Saturday, she'll get him to let her stay.'

The night had not gone well, Josephine discovered when she went on duty in the morning. The operation cases had, true enough, slept their way through the night in a drugged sleep, but everybody else had been disturbed on several occasions by Mrs Prosser, who declared herself to be dying neglected and in need of cups of tea, cold drinks and bedpans. That she had been on her feet for days now and perfectly able to get herself to the loo was an argument delivered in a fierce whisper by the night Staff Nurse, which she swept aside so noisily that they were forced to give in to her. She lay in bed now, looking smug, having declared herself incapable of getting out of her bed.

Josephine listened with a sympathetic ear to the night Staff Nurse's report and sent her and her junior off duty with a promise that something would be done before the night, and once her nurses had dispersed to see to breakfasts she asked Joan to stay behind for a few minutes.

'The side ward; the one at the other end of the ward that we don't use unless we have to—we'll put her in there. She's not to be neglected, mind, but she must get up as usual—she can sit there and have her meals there, and when Mr Bull does his round I'll see if he'll talk to her.'

Josephine supervised the move. Mrs Prosser, at first delighted at getting so much attention, became incensed when she discovered that she was to be on her own. Josephine waited until she had finished her diatribe, forcefully delivered, about the cruelty of nurses and herself above all, and then she pointed out reasonably; 'Well, Mrs Prosser, if you are feeling as poorly as you say, then I think that you should be kept as quiet as possible. I think Mr Bull will agree with me. He's doing a round later this morning and you can tell him exactly what is wrong. Your temperature and pulse are quite normal, and you ate your breakfast and you haven't been sick.'

Mrs Prosser said a rude word, but Josephine, inured to the colourful vocabulary of the majority of her patients, took not a bit of notice. She left Mrs Prosser's door half open and swept back down the ward, distinctly eye catching in her dark blue cotton uniform and frilled cap; other hospitals might dress their nurses in nylon and paper caps, St Michael's hadn't changed the material or the cut since they were first designed in the mid-nineteenth century. Perhaps they weren't as comfortable as the modern overall, but the St Michael's nurses wore them with pride and spent time getting their caps just so.

With Josephine's eye here, there and everywhere, the ward gradually assumed the perfection she expected. The ill ladies were attended to, comforted, their hair nicely combed, and set against their pillows, those who were able, got from their beds and were settled in chairs, and the in betweens, not yet quite well enough to do much for themselves, were encouraged to swing their legs out of bed, totter for little walks under the watchful eye of a nurse, and then sit up in their beds, where, feeling pleased with themselves, they read the paper or knitted. And in the meantime Joan Makepeace and a Senior Student Nurse had started the treatments and the dressings. By the time the nurses started going to their coffee the morning was successfully embarked upon its routine.

Mr Bull arrived just as Josephine, having checked that all was going well with her patients, was thinking of her own coffee. He surged into the ward, bringing a wave of good humour with him. He was accompanied by the colleague who was to do his work while he was away; the man in the car, no less. She halted for a moment, on her way down the ward to meet them, and then went on, her colour a little high, but her calm unimpaired.

Mr Bull gave her a jovial greeting, 'Jo—everything spick and span, I see—I've never managed to catch you out yet, have I? I've brought Mr

Julius van Tacx—he'll be doing my work for me
while I'm away. Julius, meet my favourite Ward
Sister, Josephine Dowling. She's getting married
very shortly, more's the pity.'

Josephine extended a large, well kept hand and
had it engulfed in an enormous grip. She said,
'How d'you do?' in a rather colourless voice and
was taken aback when he replied, carelessly.

'Oh, we have met already, haven't we?'

Mr Bull was all ears. 'Oh, where?'

'In the middle of a country road in a rainstorm.
Miss Dowling took exception to my driving.'

Mr Bull was by no means insensitive to atmosphere. He glanced at Jo's wooden countenance
and then at Mr Van Tacx's amused face and said
uneasily, 'Yes, well—I daresay you'll work very
well together. This is one of the best run wards in
the hospital.'

Mr Van Tacx bowed his head slightly in what
Josephine considered to be a mocking gesture. His,
'Of course', sounded mocking too.

She said austerely, 'Naturally I and my nursing
staff will do everything to make things as easy as
possible for Mr Van Tacx.'

'Oh, I don't expect things to be easy,' he told
her cheerfully, 'but I daresay we'll rub along.'

There was nothing to reply to this, Jo led the
way to the first bed and the round began, supported
by a posse of students, Joan Makepeace and a
Student Nurse clutching a pile of patient's notes.
It took twice as long, of course, Mr van Tacx had
to have every sign and symptom explained to him
as well as reading the foot of every bed as they

came to it. Josephine, longing for her coffee, allowed no vestige of her impatience to show, making suitable replies to the questions fired at her, producing the correct forms seconds before they were asked for, behaving in short, just as a well trained nurse ought. So much so in fact that Mr Bull paused at the end of the ward to enquire what was the matter with her. 'Swallowed the poker, Jo?' he asked, 'you don't need to be so starchy just because Mr van Tacx is here.'

Jo looked down her beautiful nose. 'I hope that I shall treat Mr Van Tacx exactly as I have always treated you, sir,' she said sweetly. 'Would you like to see Mrs Prosser? I've put her in the end side ward; she kept everyone awake last night and is convinced that she isn't well enough to go home, I suggested to her that if she were in a room by herself she might begin to feel better.'

'Oh, God—must I see her? There's nothing wrong is there?'

Josephine glanced at her notes. 'Nothing at all.'

'Oh, well in that case. . .' He caught her eye. 'You think I'd better have a word?'

She nodded and led the way to the side ward. Mrs Prosser was sitting up in her bed, waiting for them. She didn't waste time with any good-mornings, but launched her attack without preamble. They stood listening imperturbably until she stopped for lack of breath.

'Well, Mrs Prosser,' said Mr Bull, 'here is a well-known specialist who has come to examine you. I do feel that if he pronounces you fit you have no option but to take his advice and go home on Saturday.'

Josephine had to admit that Mr van Tacx handled Mrs Prosser with a masterly touch; he examined her with a thoroughness which impressed even that lady, then treated her to a brief lecture, delivered in his deep faintly accented voice, ending it with a flattering observation on her fortitude and ability to cope with any future difficulties.

Josephine, who had decided that she didn't like him, was forced to allow admiration for his handling of the difficult old lady. Leaving Mrs Prosser smirking amongst her pillows, she led the way to her office where Mr Bull waved away his retinue. He was in a good mood; coffee would take twice as long as usual, thought Josephine, which meant that she would be all behind with the paperwork. She was a calm tempered girl, and patient; she poured coffee for the three of them and sat down to drink hers at the desk while the two gentlemen disposed themselves—Mr Bull in a canvas chair in one corner of the small room, the Dutchman leaning against a radiator. There was no question of social conversation, of course. They plunged immediately into several knotty problems which had revealed themselves during the round, turning to her from time to time to verify some sticky point. It was when they got up to go at last that Mr van Tacx paused as they were going through the door.

'I shall be seeing you presently, Sister Dowling; there are one or two points we might discuss. I hope we shall enjoy a pleasant relationship.'

Josephine gave him a thoughtful look. 'I hope so, too, sir.' She hadn't much liked his silken tones. Rather childishly, she made a face at the closed door, said, 'Pooh to you,' and then drew a pile of reports towards her, only to be interrupted a moment later by the door being thrust open again to admit Mr van Tacx's handsome head.

'Shall we let bygones be bygones?' he wanted to know, and smiled at her with such charm that just for the moment she liked him very much. Before she could answer him, he had gone again, leaving her with her feelings nicely muddled.

As she might have known, he was thoroughly discussed at midday dinner. Caroline and Mercy both pronounced him dreamy. 'Such a lovely dark brown voice!' enthused the latter. 'And so good looking. Caroline, you're a lucky devil, you'll see him four times a week, besides the times he might stroll in for the odd cup of coffee.'

Caroline, a pretty girl with curly blonde hair and big baby blue eyes, smirked. 'I know. What a bit of luck Jo's out of the running—I wouldn't stand a chance, nor would you.'

'Speak for yourself.' Mercy turned a gamin little face to Jo. 'What do you say, Jo?'

'Why, that he's a man who knows his job— he'd have to or Mr Bull wouldn't let him near his patients in the first place.'

'You don't like him?'

'I don't know him, so how can I tell?' asked Jo reasonably. 'Does anyone know anything about him?'

'Not a thing. He's Dutch, qualified here as well as in Holland, lives near Leiden, had a flourishing practice and likes lots of sugar in his coffee. . .'

Josephine turned thoughtful eyes on to her friend's face. 'Not bad, considering you only met him for the first time this morning.'

'You wait a week, Jo. I must find out if he's married or got a girl. Married, I should think— he's not all that young, is he? Probably got a pack of children and a wife. . .'

'Then why isn't she with him? I mean, he's in a service flat, one of those posh ones just behind Harrods, I heard old Chubb'—Chubb was the senior porter—'telling one of the porters to take some luggage there.'

Several pairs of eyes were turned upon Mercy, who had volunteered this interesting information, and she smiled round the table. 'What's more, I heard him say that Mr van Tacx has friends in Wiltshire—Tisbury. . .' She stopped short, 'Jo, you live near there. . .'

Josephine took a mouthful of wholesome steamed pudding before she replied. 'I've met him—when I was home, you know. He passed me in his car, going towards Tisbury, but he could have been making for several villages. . .'

'How do you know it was him?'

'He stopped.' Jo treated the table to a calm stare. 'It was very wet,' she volunteered as though that was sufficient explanation.

'Lord, what a chance—and it had to be you, Jo, safely settled with your Malcolm.'

It was a pity, mused Josephine on her way back to the ward, that for some reason which she couldn't explain, she felt neither safe nor settled. It was a very good thing that Malcolm was calling for her that evening; he was a junior partner in a large practice on the fringe of Hampstead and it was his free evening. She hadn't seen him for more than a week, which was perhaps why she had this strange feeling of uncertainty about the future. Perhaps she had got into a rut, staying on at St Michael's after she had trained, thoroughly entrenched in her job and unlike some of her friends who had to help with family finances, quite comfortably off. Indeed, Malcolm had laughingly told her that she wouldn't be able to indulge her taste for expensive clothes once they were married. 'There'll be plenty of money,' he explained, 'but I don't believe in wasting it on fripperies—Mother makes a lot of her dresses, I'm sure she'll give you a hand.'

Josephine shuddered at the thought; his mother's clothes, clothing an extra outsize for a start, were as remote from fashion as the moon was from cheese. She was still frowning about it when she reached her office. Joan would be there with a tray of tea which they would share while they planned the rest of the day's work and discussed the ill patients. Visitors were already waiting impatiently outside the swing doors and during the next hour there was very little to do other than check on the post-op cases. Young Student Nurses had all been given some chores to keep them busy until the bell was rung and they could do teas. Joan would have cast an eye where necessary. She sighed for no reason at all, and opened her office door.

CHAPTER TWO

MR van Tacx was standing with his back to the door, looking out of the window at the view; the widowless wall bounding the theatre wing, separated from the gyny ward by a strip of grass supporting a plane tree. He turned round as Josephine went in so that his massive person shut out most of the daylight, and leaned against the window frame.

'Do you ever look out of the window?' he asked.

'Only if I have to. Is there something you want, sir?'

'I should like to go over the notes of the post operation cases. . .'

He paused as the door opened and Joan came in with the tea tray. She stopped short and said: 'Oh, sorry, I didn't know you were here, sir.'

She glanced at Josephine. 'Shall I get another cup, Sister?'

Josephine ignored his slow smile. 'Why, yes, Staff, and stay will you? Mr van Tacx wants some notes—Mrs Shaw, Mrs Butterworth, Miss Price and Mrs King.' She sat down at her desk and picked up some forms lying on it. 'Mrs Butterworth's Path Lab report's back.' She lifted her eyes to Mr van Tacx's impassive face. 'I daresay you took a look at it, sir.'

'No I didn't,' he said to surprise her. 'I should

dislike it very much if you were to poke around my desk, and I rather fancy you would feel the same way.' He smiled his charming smile again and she found herself smiling back.

'Oh, that's better,' he said quietly as Joan came back with the tea cup. Josephine who seldom blushed, found herself doing just that, too. But she poured the tea in her usual calm manner, laid the notes on the desk and offered her chair. He waved that aside, however, and went to sit on the radiator and sip his tea and read through the notes. Presently he held out his hand for the Path Lab report and studied that too.

'Radiotherapy, I think, don't you, Sister? Let us get her on her feet first though, so that she feels she is making good progress. You keep your patients in for that?'

'Usually; it depends on the patient. . .'

'Yes, of course. And these other ladies. . .' He passed his cup for more tea and began on the other notes. Josephine drank her own tea and watched him. She had to admit that he was very good looking but she wasn't sure if she liked his faint air of arrogance. Accustomed to getting his own way, she decided, and probably quite nasty if he didn't.

He looked up suddenly and returned her look with a long cool one of his own. He said quietly, 'I think that we must get to know each other, Sister Dowling.' And then he got up to go.

When they were alone, Joan said, 'He's nice, isn't he? I don't mean good looking and all that, he's got every nurse in the place on her toes; I'm not sure what it is but if I were in a tight corner I'd shout for him. . .'

Josephine gave her Staff Nurse a surprised look. Joan Makepeace was one of the most level headed girls she had ever met, popular with nurses and the students and housemen alike, not particularly pretty but kind and hard working and while not lacking dates, she had made it plain that she had no intention of taking anyone seriously until she had achieved what she had set out to do; have a ward of her own. She admired Josephine. Indeed, her ambition was to be exactly like her, calm and serene and able to cope with any emergency which might arise. She knew that she had a chance of getting Josephine's job when she left to marry, but genuinely regretted her going. She said carefully. 'I haven't thought about him, Joan. . .'

'Well, I don't suppose you would—I mean you've got Malcolm.'

Josephine who hadn't given Malcolm a thought for the best part of the day, agreed.

The period of quiet was over, there was still ten minutes to go before visiting time was over; Josephine went into the ward, cast a quick eye over the four operation cases, agreed to talk to their visitors presently and made her way slowly round the ward, to be stopped every few yards by relatives and friends. Some of their questions she couldn't answer, they were better dealt with by one of the surgeons; she would have to get Mr Bull's registrar, Matt Cummings to come up to the ward. But all the other questions she answered patiently and helpfully, knowing that to the people concerned they were important. Back in her office she phoned Matt and then, one by one, invited the anxious mothers and sisters and daughters to come and talk. There were never any husbands in the afternoon, they came in the evening, clutching flowers and things in paper bags and sometimes they rather shyly offered her a gift. Chocolates mostly, sometimes a bag of oranges or a melon and as Christmas approached, nuts. She accepted them with gratitude because it was nice that in the middle of what was to most men a domestic upheaval, they remembered the nurses.

Malcolm was waiting for her; she had got off duty rather later than usual and had hurried to change and make her way to the front entrance. He was standing by the entrance, reading an evening paper, and she paused, unseen as yet, to look at him. Not over tall, stoutly built, nice looking in a smug kind of way. It struck her forcibly that she couldn't possibly marry him. In ten years time he would be satisfied with his life, following in his father's footsteps, content to take over from him and probably when his father died, having his mother to live with them. . . He had never been keen on an evening out, she suspected. No, she knew now that once they were married, she would be expected to stay at home or at best visit his family. The enormity of it all shook her; she felt guilty and mean, but surely it was better to cry off now rather than go through with an unhappy marriage? And why, she asked herself miserably, should she suddenly be aware of these thing? True she had had doubts from time to time but she had supposed that was natural enough in an engaged woman, but now it wasn't doubts, it was dreadful certainty.

She walked on again and he looked up and saw her. His, 'Hullo old girl,' did nothing to reassure her, nor did the perfunctory kiss he dropped on her cheek, but she struggled to respond to it, feeling guiltier than ever so that she responded rather more warmly than usual and he drew back with a 'Hey—what's got into you, Jo?' And when she just shook her head. 'Had a busy day, no doubt— well we'll go to a cafe and have a meal; that'll set you on your feet again.'

She longed to tell him that a cafe wouldn't help in the least; champagne and an exotic dinner at some fashionable restaurant might have helped, but she doubted that even. She said urgently, 'Malcolm, could we go somewhere quiet where we can talk?'

'Quiet? Why do we want to be quiet?' He was ushering her into his car as he spoke. He added rather irritably, 'I'm not made of money, you know. . .'

A rather unfair remark, she decided, sitting silent beside him.

The restaurant was fairly full and noisy. They found a table for two and he said as they sat down. 'Steak for you?' And when she said that no she would have a poached egg on toast, he observed shortly, 'Whatever is the matter with you, Jo? I always order a steak for you. . .'

She said lamely, 'I'm not hungry, Malcolm,' and then trying hard to recapture something she knew was lost for ever, 'Have you had a busy day?'

'Oh, God, yes. I'll be glad to be shot of the Hampstead practice, there'll be just enough to keep me busy with Father, there's nothing like a country practice—one knows everyone in the district, a settled routine. . .

'Is that what you want, Malcolm? Don't you want to—to stretch your wings? Use your knowledge?'

He laughed. 'Jo, you're not yourself this evening, what on earth's got into you. Why should I want to wear myself out when I can drop into a comfortable country practice with my father?'

She abandoned the egg on toast. She was appalled to hear herself say, 'Malcolm, I don't want to get married.'

He finished his mouthful before he replied. 'Rubbish, Jo. You're just tired—you don't know what you are saying.'

She said doggedly, 'But I do. I—I've felt uncertain for a week or two but I thought—well I thought I'd get over it, but I haven't, Malcolm. I'd make you a bad wife—there are all sorts of reasons—living so far away and being so near your parents. Your mother doesn't like me much, you know that; she thinks I'm too keen on clothes and don't know enough about keeping house, and I want to do more than just be a housewife—and I'm not sure that I love you enough, Malcolm.' She paused and went on bravely. 'I'm not even sure if you love me enough. You see, I think, perhaps you're mistaken in me—I don't like being told what to do and being taken for granted. Why do I have to eat steak when we go out just because you think I want to? Can't you see that if you expect me to eat steak because you order it for me, you'll expect me to do everything else you think is good for me.'

Malcolm gave an indulgent laugh, which infuriated her. 'You are just being silly, Jo. Good Lord, we're to be married in a couple of months, you can't break everything off now.'

'You mean to tell me that you think we should go ahead with the wedding even when I know in my heart that I don't want to marry you?'

He shrugged. 'You'll feel differently in the morning. Besides, what will everyone say. . .'

'They'd say a lot more if I ran away after we were married.'

'You don't mean that. Why do women have to exaggerate so?'

She saw that she wasn't going to get through his smugness. She said soberly, 'I'm not exaggerating, Malcolm, I mean every word.' And she took the ring off her finger and pushed it across the table towards him. 'Please will you take me back to St Michael's.'

He picked up the ring and put it in his pocket. 'If that's how you feel, the quicker we part company the better. You're not the girl I thought you were.'

She agreed sadly, 'You'll meet some girl who'll make you happy, Malcolm. I'm very sorry, but it's far better to part than to be unhappy for the rest of our lives.'

He muttered something, and because she was a kind-hearted girl and blamed herself she was honest and said so, to be brought up short by his, 'Oh save that, I'm beginning to think that once I've got over the awkwardness of it all, it'll be a good thing.'

He paid the bill and they went out to the car and got in without speaking. They still hadn't said a word when he drew up at the Hospital entrance.

Josephine opened her door. 'Well, goodbye, Malcolm—I'm sorry. . .'

He presented an unmoved profile to her. 'I doubt that,' he told her, and caught the door and slammed it shut and drove away without another word.

She stood for a moment watching the tail lights receding and then pushed the glass swing doors open. Mr van Tacx was standing just inside, barring her path.

'Hullo,' he observed 'had a tiff?'

It was a bit too much; Josephine lifted a pale face to his, blinking back tears. 'What do you know about tiffs?' She asked him bitterly and sped past him, intent on getting to her room so that she could have a really good cry.

It was a good thing that most of her friends were out for the evening or had retired to their beds. She lay in a very hot bath, crying her eyes out, and then as red as a lobster and quite worn out, got into her bed. She had expected to stay awake all night, but she fell asleep at once and didn't wake until she was called in the morning. Nothing could disguise her swollen eyelids or her still pink nose; she did the best she could with make-up and was grateful when her friends said nothing at breakfast even though they cast covert glances at her.

It was perhaps a good thing that her day turned out to be so busy that she had no time to spare for herself; there was no sign of Mr van Tacx, which considering his nasty remark on the previous evening, was a good thing, but Matt did a round, pronounced himself satisfied, declared himself delighted that Mrs Prosser would be leaving them in the morning and had a cup of coffee before he went away again. But not before he had stopped on his way out of the ward to speak to Joan. Josephine, coming out of her office behind him, saw Joan's pink face and her smile; whatever the girl said, she couldn't hide the pleasure at whatever Matt was saying. Bereft of her own romance, Josephine was delighted to see another blossoming under her nose. Matt was quiet and solid and nothing much to look at, but he was a clever surgeon; Joan would suit him admirably. Josephine went on down the ward, already busy with plans to arrange the off duty so that Joan would be free when Matt had his half days.

The next day they admitted three patients for operations on the morrow; Mrs Prior, a timid little lady with an overbearing husband who button-holed Josephine and demanded to know just exactly what was to be done to his wife. She asked him mildly if his own doctor hadn't already explained it to him.

'Corse 'e 'as. But 'oos ter believe 'im, eh? The

missus ain't all that ill, and 'oo's ter look after me?'

'You?' said Josephine gently. 'Most husbands manage very well. I'll get one of the surgeons to see you if you like. Your wife will have her operation in the morning and you can 'phone about one o'clock and come round in the evening and talk to someone about her.'

She was glad to see him go and she suspected that his wife, meek though she was, was just as glad. The other two ladies were easier to deal with; both married and middle aged with worried husbands anxious to do the right thing. She put their minds at rest and when they had gone went along to have a little chat with the three women. Mr Bull had fallen into the habit of letting her describe their operations to his patients; most of them wanted to know exactly what would be done and more importantly, if it was going to hurt. Josephine reassured them, gave them a clear idea of what the surgeon intended doing and suggested that they should get themselves unpacked, bathed and into bed, ready for the House Surgeon to examine them. He was new to the team, enthusiastic about his work and tended to frighten the patients by his sheer earnestness. Josephine took care to be with him so that she could tone down some of his more frank remarks. Frankness, she felt, should be left to the registrar, or better still, the consultant gynaecologist.

The next morning, being theatre day, was busy, but after the trauma of getting Mrs Prosser away Josephine welcomed the business with relief.

Doctor Macauley, the anaesthetist, had seen the patients on the previous evening and now they lay in their beds, looking strangely alike in their white theatre gowns and caps. Mrs Prior was to go first, Josephine drew up the pre med, and went along to Mrs Prior, lying meekly, waiting uncomplainingly for whatever was about to happen to her. She slowed her steps as the ward door at the far end opened and Mr van Tacx came unhurriedly in. He was dressed impeccably, the very picture of a successful consultant in his dark grey suit and subdued tie and he brought with him a distinct air of assurance and at the same time a feeling of ordinariness so that the three ladies, waiting, outwardly calm and inwardly wishing with all their hearts that they might jump out of their beds and go home, were instantly put at rest. His 'good morning, Sister', was uttered in the casual tones of one greeting the milkman on his round and when he sat down on the end of Mrs Prior's bed, she gave him a look which Josephine could only describe to herself as adoring.

He talked to each one of them in turn, in a calm, pleasant voice which she could only admire. The thought crossed her mind that if she had to have an operation at any time, then Mr van Tacx would do very nicely for the surgeon. The three ladies obviously felt the same way, for they smiled and nodded and Mrs Prior hardly noticed when she slid the pre med, into her arm.

Josephine took them to the theatre, leaving Joan in charge, something she had started when she had taken over the ward, for she had discovered soon enough that the patients, semi-conscious as they were, were wheeled away with quieter minds if they knew that she was with them. Once in the aneasthetic room and the patient out cold within seconds of the anaesthetist's skilful insertion of the needle, she handed over to a Senior Student Nurse.

She felt regret at having to do this, she would dearly have loved to have watched Mr van Tacx operating. She went back to the ward and set about the daily routine until they 'phoned from the Recovery Room to say that Mrs Prior was ready to be fetched and would she send up the next case please.

She whisked the next lady up to the anaesthetic room; a placid person, already half asleep and uncaring, and then went to supervise the return of Mrs Prior.

Mrs Prior seemed to have shrunk, her small pale face smaller and paler than ever. Josephine received her instructions from Fiona, the recovery room Sister, nodded briskly and saw her safely back to the ward and into her bed, detailing a student nurse to take fifteen minute observations and report if she was worried. 'And you nip off to dinner,' she told Joan, 'and take Nurse Thursby and Nurse Williams with you, there's still Mrs Gregory to go up but she's a straightforward Colpol: and Mrs Clark shouldn't take more than an hour. With luck we'll be clear by five o'clock. . .'

'Your dinner, Sister?'

'Oh, I'll have a sandwich and a pot of tea later on.'

The day wore on, Mrs Clark came back, smiled

vaguely at Josephine as she gave her an injection and she went peacefully to sleep, leaving her free to do a round of her patients and check Mrs Prior once more. There was a little colour in her cheeks now and Josephine checked the blood transfusion and cast an eye over the nurse's observation board. Joan was back by now with the two nurses, and Josephine sent the Senior Student Nurse to her dinner; she would have to wait for her own pot of tea; Mrs Gregory had been gone for some time and she must be on the ward when she came back.

They rang shortly afterwards and she went along to collect her patient; 'straightforward,' whispered Fiona, 'and what a duck Mr van Tacx was to work for. Lucky you,' she added and winked over her mask.

'That's as maybe,' hissed Josephine peevishly, 'I want a meal—I missed coffee and it's gone two o'clock.'

'We stopped for coffee after Mrs Prior,' said Fiona smugly. 'and I managed a sandwich before Mrs Gregory.'

Josephine was getting that lady settled in her bed and giving instructions to Nurse Thursby at the same time. A good little nurse, reliable but uncertain of herself. She listened now, repeating Josephine's instructions rather apprehensively.

'And don't be scared,' begged Josephine, 'the bell's there, I or Staff will come at once and in any case I'll be popping in and out to see how things are.'

She became aware that Nurse Thursby's eye had strayed to a spot behind her and looked over her shoulder. Mr van Tacx was there, immaculate again just as though he hadn't spent the morning in theatre gear and rubber boots. Indeed, he had all the appearance of a prosperous stockbroker or something executive in the city, accustomed to a pen in his hand and not the scalpel. He nodded to Josephine, smiled at Nurse Thursby and bent over his patient, who opened her eyes blearily and closed them again.

'She's had her morphia?'

'Not yet, sir,' Josephine's voice was quiet but it had a faint edge. 'Mrs Gregory has just returned to the ward and been put to bed.'

He nodded again. 'The other two?'

Josephine went with him to Mrs Clark, still peacefully sleeping and then to Mrs Prior. He stood for a minute looking at her, read her chart, took her pulse and held the curtain aside for Josephine to go past him.

'Your office, Sister?'

She led the way, pausing to tell Joan to give Mrs Gregory her injection. Despite her busy day she looked serene and very beautiful, even if a little untidy about the head.

In the office she sat down behind her desk and Mr van Tacx sat down cautiously in the canvas chair which sagged and creaked under his weight.

'Could we have a pot of tea?' he enquired. 'It's rather late for lunch and I have a teaching round in half an hour.'

She beamed at him. 'I'm so glad you've asked. I missed coffee and dinner too. Just a sec.'

She left him sitting and crossed the landing to

the kitchen where Mrs Cross the ward orderly was getting the tea trolley ready for the patients teas. She looked up as Josephine went in and left the trolley to turn the gas up under the kettle. 'Not 'ad yer dinner,' she said accusingly, 'I can 'ear yer stomach rumbling from 'ere. Tea and a sandwich or two—you go back ter the office and I'll bring it.'

'You're a dear, Mrs Cross, and could you put on another cup and saucer? Mr van Tacx missed his lunch and he's famished as well as thirsty.'

'Is 'e now? A fine body of a man like 'im needs 'is food. If yer was to ring them so-and-so's in the kitchen, they could send up a bit of 'am.'

Mr van Tacx was lying back at his ease with his eyes shut. Josephine lifted the receiver but he didn't open them.

'Mr van Tacx has missed his lunch. Will you send up some ham for sandwiches please, right away. . .'

'Cheese?' He asked softly with his eyes still shut.

'And cheese,' she added firmly, 'and please be quick; he has a teaching round very shortly.'

'I can see that we are going to get on very well together.' His eyes were still closed.

'I hope so, sir.'

He opened one eye. 'A whole month; do you suppose we shall be able to keep this affability up?'

She gave him a wary look. 'I cannot see why not, sir.'

'I hope that if and when we meet out of working

hours, you will refrain from addressing me as sir.'

'If you wish that—but we are very unlikely to meet.'

'There is a divinity that shapes our ends, rough hew them how we may.' He opened the other eye. 'Your William Shakespeare, or to put it more simply. "Nothing is so certain as the unexpected".'

And while she was still staring at him.

'Mrs Prior. . .' He was businesslike now. 'I'm afraid we may be too late there but we'll do what we can. She is married? Husband? Children?'

'A husband. There's a son in Australia.'

'Would she be cared for if we sent her home?'

'I doubt it. Mr Prior was concerned about himself when he talked to me. He may have been worried, of course.'

'I'll see him. If necessary we'll send her to a convalescent home and she can come back for radiotheraphy in a week or two.'

Mrs Cross came in then, bearing a loaded tray which she dumped on to Josephine's desk. 'There yer are, Sister, there's enough for the pair of yer— as nice a bit of 'am as I seen for a long time and real cheese, not that stuff they send us for the diabetics when we 'ave 'em. On account of you being important,' she explained kindly to Mr van Tacx who was looking at her with a fascinated eye. 'Now eat up and there's more tea if yer fancy it.'

Josephine thanked her and when Mrs Cross had gone said demurely, 'She doesn't mean to be familiar—she's above rubies and has been here for heaven knows how many years. She has never gone on strike or gone slow and once or twice when there's been a flap on, she'll just stay in the kitchen making tea to keep us going.'

She poured the tea, a strong, dark brew which she milked generously before she passed it with the sugar bowl.

Mr van Tacx helped himself lavishly and sipped appreciatively. 'I have acquired the habit of drinking tea,' he remarked. 'In Holland we drink coffee and tea is milkless and much weaker. This would drive a train.'

He settled into his chair and Josephine said severely, 'If you don't sit still the chair is going to collapse. Have a sandwich.'

They sat for a moment in a pleasant companionship but presently Mr van Tacx started to discuss the patients and Josephine became at once a Ward Sister who knew exactly what was expected of her. She replenished their cups, passed the sandwiches to his side of the desk and got out her pen; like Mr Bull, he fired off instructions at an alarming rate and she couldn't hold all of them in her head.

Presently he got up to go. 'I'll be in later,' he told her, 'and ring down to the lodge when Mr Prior gets here. You're on this evening?'

She didn't tell him that she should have been off duty at five o'clock but as so often happened on theatre day, she had stayed on duty.

'Yes,' she said quietly, 'I'm on until eight o'clock, Mr van Tacx, and I'll 'phone down for you. But will you be here?'

He said coldly, 'Did I not make myself clear, Sister?'

A remark which effectively wiped away the faint liking she had begun to admit to.

At supper, when she was at last off duty, several of her friends wanted to know why she hadn't gone off duty. 'How's that new man?' they wanted to know. 'Slow?'

She shook her head. 'Oh, no, but the first case took about twice as long as he had expected and then I stayed on because that particular patient's husband was coming to visit. He was a bit difficult yesterday. Mr van Tacx came up to see him. . .'

'And what's Malcolm going to say to that?' asked a voice, 'staying on duty just to oblige a consultant and him too good looking to be true.' The speaker sighed gustily. 'I wouldn't mind being in your shoes, Jo. . .'

Josephine put her knife and fork carefully together on her plate. She didn't like the girl who spoke; the Medical Ward Sister, a good nurse but spiteful at times. You can jump in any time you like,' she said calmly, 'for my part you can have carte blanche, and as for Malcolm, since we are no longer engaged, he has no say in the matter.'

She got up from the table and walked out of the canteen and the hapless girl who had spoken was attacked from all sides. To her cries that she hadn't known and she hadn't meant any harm anyway she met with a forthright warning to hold her silly tongue in future and mind her own business.

Josephine went to her room, took off her cap, wrapped a tweed coat over her uniform, pulled her leather boots over her black tights, and left the nurses home by the side door nearest the car park used by the staff. She wasn't very clear as to what she intended to do or where she was going: it was already dark, a nasty blustery evening and chilly. She wanted above all things to go home but that was too far. She unlocked the Mini and got into the driver's seat and sat there, her mind a miserable blank.

'And where are you going?' asked Mr van Tacx gently, and poked his head through the open window.

She had let out a squeak of fright which she covered in a dignified but breathless, 'Out, Mr van Tacx, and I do not care to have the wits scared out of me. . .'

'Sorry.' He sounded not in the least sorry and he made no attempt to remove his head from the window. 'Feeling low, aren't you? It's unpleasant to be jilted. . .' She muttered furiously and he went on calmly, 'Oh, several persons have told me, you're a nine days wonder you know. You'll get over it.'

'I do not care to discuss my affairs with you, Mr van Tacx and I cannot think of what possible interest they can be to you anyway.'

'Well, no—why should you? All you really need now is a shoulder to weep into and someone to listen. I haven't felt the need of a shoulder myself but I'm willing to lend you mine—you'll feel better when you've talked about it.'

She said furiously, 'How could you possibly know?'

'Because I've been jilted myself.' He opened the door. 'Move over, I'll drive somewhere where we can have coffee or a drink.'

She opened her mouth to refuse, realised that it would be useless anyway and found herself squashed into the other seat. The small part of her brain that wasn't numbed by surprise, noted that a Mini really wasn't a car for a man of his size.

'Do you mind where we go?' He didn't wait for her to answer. 'Is the tank full?'

'Yes.'

'Good. We'll keep to this side of town shall we? Do you know Epping Forest? Buckhurst Hill—the Roebuck—we can get something there.'

He didn't speak as the took the little car through Hackney and on to the dreary bricks of Leyton and Wanstead, but then going north towards Epping Forest, he began to talk. Later she couldn't remember what he had said, but his voice had been pleasantly soothing and she had relaxed. By the time they reached the Roebuck she had pulled herself together, even felt a little ashamed of herself. Next time, she promised herself, she would be armed against being taken unawares, and anyway, by the morning the whole Hospital would know. . .

The pub was very much to her taste, actually a country hotel with a comfortable bar nicely filled. Mr van Tacx parked the Mini and marched her briskly inside and sat her down at a table in a quiet corner.

'Coffee and a brandy with it and sandwiches?'

She nodded, suddenly remembering that she was still in uniform and that she had done nothing to her hair or her face. It was disconcerting when he observed, 'You look quite all right and no one can see the uniform.'

He wandered off then to the bar and came back presently with coffee and the brandy, followed a moment later by a plump smiling girl with the sandwiches.

'I went to supper,' said Josephine.

'Did you eat anything?'

'Well, no. . .'

'Eat up, we can't have you wilting away while Mr Bull's gone—I need all the help I can get.'

She didn't believe that; he looked the kind of man who would never need help, certainly not with his work. She said, searching for a safe topic, 'There's a long waiting list. . .'

'I know'. He bit into a sandwich. 'Drink your brandy. What do you intend to do?'

Her eyes watered as she sipped. 'What do you mean?'

'Don't be a dim girl. Get him back? Forget him and dedicate yourself to nursing for ever and ever? Or turn your back on him and start again? There are plenty of fish in the sea, you know, and you've the looks to pick and choose.'

Later on, she thought, when she had the time to think about it, his words were going to annoy her very much, but at the moment nothing seemed quite real. She took a sip of coffee to counteract the brandy and said with dignity, 'I prefer not to discuss it with you. I appreciate your kindness in bringing me here, I really do, but my—my private life can be of no interest to you. . .'

'Don't be so priggish. What you mean to say

is mind your own business. How old are you?'

Really, there was no end to the man's arrogance. 'Twenty-five almost twenty-six.' She hadn't meant to answer him, normally she wouldn't have done but she wasn't quite herself, it was, after all, only five days since she and Malcolm had split up and somehow the hurt of it was biting deeper now than it had done to begin with. She had her mouth open to remind him that that wasn't his business either when he observed casually, 'At least you're not an impetuous young girl,' and ignoring her affronted glance at this, 'I'm thirty-four, a good age for a man to marry should he find the right girl.'

Josephine bit into another sandwich. Temper had sharpened her appetite;

'That sounds very cold blooded. . .'

'Indeed not, I enjoy female companionship, I enjoyed too, falling head over heels in love; unfortunately the young lady in question threw me over for a man with rather more worldly goods than I. . .'

Josephine asked the obvious question. 'Was she pretty?'

'Delightfully so.'

'And—and you loved her very much?'

'Very much.'

She was a kind-hearted girl. She said warmly, 'I'm sorry, I really am, you must feel awful.'

'One learns to live with it.' He got up. 'I'll get more coffee.' She watched him cross to the bar. He didn't look like a man with a broken heart, but she supposed that he was a man who kept his feelings hidden. She sipped the rest of her brandy and felt it warm her cold insides. It loosened her tongue too. She said chattily as he sat down, 'I don't suppose that's why, you're so—so... You were awfully rude when we met—I daresay you hate all women. I didn't like you, you know, I'm not sure if I do now.'

She drank some coffee; perhaps she shouldn't have said that. She glanced at Mr van Tacx, staring at her from across the table, and was reassured to see that he was smiling. All the same she said uncertainly, 'I didn't mean to be rude,' and then like a child, 'I'm not used to drinking brandy.'

His voice was bland. 'You'll sleep well after it. Drink your coffee, we're going back.'

She felt pleasantly tired as he drove away from the Roebuck. She closed her eyes and slept soundly until he stopped the car in the car park, and lifted her head from the shoulder she had rested it on. He studied her sleeping face for a few moments before setting her upright, smiling faintly. He said briskly, 'Wake up, Josephine...'

She opened her eyes at once and blinked round and then at him. 'Oh, we're back—I'm sorry, I fell asleep. Oh, dear, what must you think...'

He leaned over and opened her door. 'Jump out while I lock the car.'

He sounded abrupt and she made haste to do as he asked and then took the keys from him. 'Thank-you,' she began in a rush, 'I do appreciate your kindness...'

He then looked at her unsmiling. 'Good night,

Josephine!' And when he had nothing more to say, she stood uncertainly for a moment and then went away.

CHAPTER THREE

EATING a hasty breakfast the next morning, she came to the conclusion that she felt a bit shy about meeting Mr van Tacx again, a needless worry, as it turned out, for he made a lengthy round during the morning and never once was his manner anything other than remotely pleasant. The round finished, he and Matt spent ten minutes drinking coffee in the office while they changed treatments and drugs, discussed the next intake and gave Josephine instructions as they did so. And when they finally went he gave her a cool stare which left her feeling quite indignant. He might at least have smiled just once. After all, they had exchanged confidences on the previous evening—at least, she amended, most of it had been on her part although he had been full of advice.

She thumped a pile of charts on to the desk. Well, she wouldn't take a word of it, she would do exactly as she wanted, she might even, if Malcolm saw fit to apologise, consider marrying him after all. . .

Even as she thought this, she knew in her heart that she would do no such thing and in any case, hadn't he said that she wasn't the girl he had thought she was? He couldn't have loved her. . .
'There is no good crying over spilt milk,' said Josephine.

It was her weekend off at the end of the week; it seemed interminable, the days dragging themselves slowly from morning to evening and at the same time almost impossibly busy. Mr van Tacx came and went, stalking through the ward with Matt at his heels and Josephine making a third. He had little to say to her and that about the patients. It was as if they had never met outside the ward; she must have annoyed him in some way she decided, and she told herself that it did not matter in the least. Knowing quite well that it did, even though her heart was broken because Malcolm didn't want to marry her. That wasn't true either, it was she who had broken off their engagement; she felt quite guilty when she remembered that; when she got home she would explain it all to her mother and see what she had to say.

Operation day went off tolerably well but Mrs Prior worried her. She wasn't picking up at all; she should have been out of bed by now, walking around a bit, taking an interest in her hair and face and swapping gossip with the other ladies. She did none of these things though, but lay quietly in bed, neither reading nor knitting, not repelling the other patients attempts at a chat, but certainly not encouraging them. It worried Josephine and she confided in Matt who must have in his turn, confided in Mr van Tacx for after the round on Friday he went straight to the Office, sat down in the canvas chair, and said, 'Now, Mrs Prior—I understand you're not happy about her?'

'No, I'm not, sir. I can't put a finger on it but she doesn't seem to mind if she gets well or not.'

'Husband?'

'He comes most evenings but never speaks to any of us.'

'Make an appointment with him, will you? Monday evening, I'll come here if you will give me a ring when he arrives.'

'Very well, sir.'

'She may not want to go home. Try and find out, will you? If that's the case we'll get her into a convalescent home. She's not due for radiotherapy yet, is she?'

'No, another two weeks. . .'

She refilled his cup and offered the biscuit tin to Matt. He took one and asked, 'Off this weekend, Jo?'

For some reason she hadn't wanted Mr van Tacx to know that. She said guardedly, 'Well, yes,' and then hurriedly, 'How's the baby, Matt?'

A happy turn in the conversation: Matt spent a minute or so describing his small nephew's first tooth, before picking up his pen to write Mr van Tacx's instructions on the pile of charts before him. Josephine, peeping at his absorbed face, thought that he hadn't heard her anyway.

She caught an evening train and less than two hours later was hurrying down the platform at Tisbury to where her father was waiting. It was a raw evening, already dark and overcast, but as far as she was concerned it could snow or blow a gale; to be home, in any weather, was bliss.

They drove the few miles from Tisbury, through the narrow high hedged lanes with Cuthbert's head thrust between them. In answer to her father's query as to her week's work, she admitted that they had been busy, 'And how about you, Father?' she wanted to know.

'Oh, the usual at this time of the year, my dear; chests and varicose veins and one or two cases of 'flu—quite nasty ones. . .'

They were still arguing amicably over a 'flu epidemic when they reached the house and while her father put the car away she hurried into the kitchen with Cuthbert hard on her heels. Her mother was there stirring something in a saucepan and Josephine sniffed delightedly 'onion soup and something tasty in the oven'. She hugged her mother. 'It's heaven to be home.'

'And lovely to see you, darling. Where's your Father?'

'Putting the car in the garage. I'll take up my bag. . .'

'Supper's ready.' Her mother looked at her. 'Tired, Jo?' Her eye fell on her daughter's ringless hand but she didn't say anything.

'Five minutes—I'll start dishing up.'

They had eaten supper and Josephine and her mother were washing the dishes while her father caught up with the paper work before Mrs Dowling said, 'You're not wearing your ring, Jo?'

It was the opening she had been waiting for but now that she had it it was hard to begin. She stacked plates carefully. 'Well, no Mother. I—I was going to tell you and Father. We—that is I, decided that we didn't suit each other. I've left it a bit late, haven't I? Only three months from the date we'd fixed, but somehow I couldn't go on with it. I thought I loved Malcolm, truly I did, but last time, when I was home out walking with Cuthbert I suddenly knew that I didn't want to marry him, so I told him.' She sighed. 'He was angry but he had every right to be. Just for a few days I felt awful, I mean, I'd got used to the idea of getting married.

Her mother cleaned a saucepan with care. 'Well, darling, if it's any consolation to you, neither your father nor I were quite happy about you marrying Malcolm. He's a nice man, we like him, but we weren't sure about you living with his parents—we've only met them once, haven't we? We liked his father but I can't say that we took to his mother.' She added thoughtfully, 'She wears such ghastly clothes and she told me how to cook cabbage—as though I didn't know. . .'

Mrs Dowling looked as indignant as a person of her gentle disposition could and Josephine laughed a little. 'And Malcolm wanted me to make my own clothes—and he said his mother would show me how. . .'

For no reason at all she burst into tears and her mother said bracingly, 'Heaven forbid,' put down the saucepan and put her arms round her daughter. 'Look, love, I know you feel bad about it but you did the right thing—you feel sore and a bit lost and it's no good my telling you that you'll look back on this in a couple of months and be glad that you did what you've done now. It was a pity you couldn't come straight home, but never mind that now; you can walk your legs off tomorrow and in the evening we've been asked to Branton

House—dinner—Lady Forsyth wanted to know if you'd be at home and I said yes. . .'

'I've nothing to wear.' Josephine sniffed and blew her beautiful nose.

Her mother picked up the saucepan again. 'I took my grey dress in to be cleaned last week; I remembered you had a stain on that rose crêpe of yours and I took it along at the same time. It looks as good as new.' She put the pan in the cupboard. 'It's such a pretty dress.' She added gently, 'You have to put a brave face on, Jo, Lady Forsyth's sure to tell other people so you won't have to do more than tell her; she's a gossip but nice with it. And the sooner they all know the easier it will be; thank heaven there aren't presents to return.'

Josephine managed a watery giggle. 'Mother, you're being so practical and I never thought you were. All right, I'll come with you tomorrow— will there be a lot of people there? Is it one of their mammoth parties?'

'No—just a few friends,' she said, 'and we all know them all.'

Josephine went up to her room and the doctor poked his head round the kitchen door. 'It's all off—Jo and Malcolm,' hissed his wife.

The doctor came all the way in. 'Does Jo mind very much? Is she upset?'

'I don't think so; she's hurt and she feels lost and it's awkward just for a bit, you know, telling everyone. . .'

'I'll get up a bottle of claret,' observed the doctor. 'It'll cheer her up.'

The claret helped, but what really helped more

was the unspoken understanding from her father and mother; she slept soundly that night and woke feeling that the world wasn't such a bad place after all.

She walked a long way the next afternoon, the faithful Cuthbert plodding along beside her, recent rain and wind had brought the leaves tumbling down and the lanes were strewn with them. But the country looked lovely, yellow and gold and tumbling clouds rushing across a pale blue sky. Josephine walked until the sky began to darken and then took the short cuts she had known since childhood which brought her home just nicely in time for tea. A light tea, her mother pointed out; Lady Forsyth had a splendid cook and it was only kind to do full justice to her efforts. Josephine, feeling peckish got into the rose crêpe and surveyed her person in the pier glass. There was a little too much of her, she considered, but what there was, was pleasant on the eye. The dress was beautifully cut and a splendid foil to her hair. She delved into her cupboard and dragged out the brown velvet evening coat she had had for years and went downstairs.

Her father was already in the sitting room, elegant in his elderly dinner jacket, catching up on the latest copy of *The Lancet*. He glanced up as she went in, said 'nice' and went on reading. Presently he said, 'Your Mother is going to be late. . .'

Josephine took the hint and went back up the nice old oak staircase to encourage her mother. Mrs Dowling was ready except for a vital zip fastening on her dress. Josephine dealt with it, found her mother's evening purse, helped her into the elderly fur coat which came out year after year, and led the way downstairs again. Cuthbert and the cat followed them to the door, looking hard done by; they hated to be left, especially in the evening, when they could be sure of laps to sit on while Cuthbert slept on his rug. During the day it didn't matter; Mrs Bragg, who came each day, could be relied upon to provide food and comfort. She and Cuthbert and the cat were all getting elderly together and understood each other very well.

Branton House, lights streaming from most of it's windows, looked imposing. It was imposing inside too, with an elderly butler to take their coats and show them to the drawingroom. Josephine, following her mother through the double doors, saw that there were ten or twelve people there. Her glance swept the room; she knew them all too. She even knew, heaven help her, Mr van Tacx, and how he had got there she couldn't even begin to guess.

He was standing at the other end of the long room, talking to Wendy Forsythe, the daughter of the house and a friend of Josephine. Whoever had thought up dinner jackets, thought Josephine, must have had him in mind; his clothes were always the epitome of perfection; in a dinner jacket he wasn't to be faulted. He was such a large man too, yet everything fitted and at the same time there was nothing flamboyant; indeed, one might say the very reverse. Josephine greeting her host and hostess, did the rounds, kissing and being kissed, until she got to Wendy and Mr van Tacx.

'Jo,' cried Wendy, 'it's ages since I saw you. I do wish you'd have a holiday and stay at home for a week or two. This is Julius van Tacx—he's a surgeon. . .'

Josephine offered a hand. 'We've met,' she said calmly. 'He's at St Michael's while Mr Bull is away.'

Wendy was delighted. 'Oh, good, you'll have plenty to talk about while I go and talk to that tiresome. . .' She stopped and bit her lip. 'Sorry, I shouldn't have said that—mother's guests and all that. . .'

'I'll not tell on you,' said Josephine, 'and Mr van Tacx, being a surgeon, is a model of discretion.'

Wendy grinned at them both and skipped away. 'How did you get here?' demanded Josephine.

He looked down at her through lazy lids. He began to say something and then changed his mind and said mildly. 'My mother went to school with Lady Forsyth.'

Josephine's generous mouth opened slightly. 'Heavens, who would have thought that. . .'

'Why not?' He was amused.

'Well, men like you. . .' She floundered a little, 'That is, your kind of man—one never imagines them having mothers and fathers and family.'

'What an interesting idea. Why not?'

'I don't mean to be rude,' she assured him earnestly, 'it's just that you don't look as though you needed anyone.'

'Then I must plead exception to the rule.' He smiled at her. 'And how's that broken heart?' He wanted to know. The sudden change in the conversation took her by surprise. She went pink and her eyes widened with indignation. 'Well—well,' she managed, and fought to get her breathing back to normal. 'Of all the beastly things to say. I hope— I hope that you break your heart one day—that is if you've got one, which I very much doubt.'

He was still smiling, which annoyed her very much. 'You really are a most interesting girl,' he observed mildly. 'To look at you, you are serene and very pretty—beautiful when you're roused and your voice is soft and charming—and yet here you are, spitting fire and vengence at me, a veritable virago.' He looked over her shoulder. 'We were discussing human nature,' he remarked smoothly to a tall thin woman who had joined them—the tiresome lady Wendy had been entertaining. 'A most interesting subject, Mrs Taylor, and of course, we see a good deal of it in hospital.'

'I daresay you two have a good deal in common.' Mrs Taylor's sharp little eyes darted from one to the other. 'Josephine, how flushed you are.'

Before she could reply, 'We were just remarking that it was warm in here,' said Mr van Tacx at his most bland. Josephine sipping her sherry had to admire the adroit way in which he guided the conversation into neutral channels despite Mrs Taylor's efforts to probe. Presently he said, 'Josephine, I should like you to take me to

meet your mother and father. Perhaps there is time
before dinner. . .'

He took his leave from Mrs Taylor with such
suave charm that Josephine was speechless with
admiration. She allowed herself to be led to the
other end of the room where her mother was talking to the rector's wife, and that lady paused in
mid-sentence to say, 'Julius, how nice to see
you—have you come to talk to Mrs Dowling? I'll
leave you then; I promised to give Lady Forsyth
the recipe for sloe gin.'

Mr van Tacx's eyebrows rose and he looked
wicked for a moment and then as Josephine introduced him became his usual charming urbane self.

'I've heard about you,' observed Mrs Dowling
pleasantly. 'Oh, not from Jo, of course, but everyone in the village knows about you.' She smiled
at him. 'You wouldn't expect rector's wives to
know about sloe gin, would you, she's a dab
hand at it.'

He gave her an appreciative grin. 'Oh, dear, did
I look so taken aback?'

'Just the eyebrows. Do you like working
with Jo?'

'Mother,' interpolated Josephine. 'I'm sure Mr
van Tacx won't want to answer that until I've
gone away.'

'On the contrary.' He put out a hand and took
a gentle grip of her arm.

'Yes, I like working with Josephine, Mrs
Dowling; she's a very competent nurse.'

Mrs Dowling beamed at him and put out a hand
to catch her husband's sleeve as he wandered

towards them. 'John, come and meet Mr van Tacx; Jo works for him, isn't that nice?'

Dr Dowling cast a quick look at his daughter's cross face. He said in a neutral kind of voice: 'Ah, yes, of course, you're the man taking over from Jack Bull, aren't you? Someone was telling me that you're trying a different incision. . .' The two men, with a muttered apology to mother and daughter, wandered off to a quiet corner.

'He's nice,' said Mrs Dowling, 'is he married?'

Josephine eyed her parent with faint exasperation. 'Mother, I do not know, and I don't want to.' Which was a fib, anyway, but it didn't seem right to pass on Mr van Tacx's problematic love life at that moment.

'Well, I daresay we shall see more of him,' observed Mrs Dowling cheerfully, 'I'll ask him—when the ice is broken, you know.'

Josephine forebore from warning her mother that Mr van Tacx could be very icy upon occasion; it would need a good deal of chipping to get to the heart of him.

There was a kind of rustle among the people in the room as Lady Forsyth's butler announced dinner, and that lady began pairing off her guests.

When she reached Josephine she said happily, 'How nice that you know Julius, dear. So suitable—I mean you can talk about whatever nurses and doctors talk about, can't you?'

Not at dinner, thought Josephine, meekly allowing herself to be paired off with Mr van Tacx, who gave her a small smile and murmured, 'Inevitable, I'm afraid, Josephine.'

She had old Mr Stone, a retired solicitor, on her other side. He was hard of hearing and liked his food, a combination which made conversation rather a labour. But she wasn't the only unlucky one; she was pleased to see that Mrs Taylor had been seated on the other side of Mr van Tacx.

They were half way through the roast duck and black cherry sauce before she and Mr van Tacx exchanged a word. His question surprised her, 'When do you go back?'

'Tomorrow evening, why?'

'I'll drive you. We'll stop for a meal on the way.'

She opened her grey eyes wide. 'Oh, am I being invited or is this a command?'

He smiled. 'You're very prickly. I thought it might be a good idea to get to know each other.'

'Why?'

He didn't answer that but said instead, 'I like your Mother. You have her eyes. Your father has a deep interest in gyny work, hasn't he?'

'Yes—he intended to specialise when he qualified but he injured a hand which prevented him operating.'

'He's been a GP ever since?'

'Yes—he came here before I was born, an aunt left him the house and the local doctor had just died.'

She had to turn back to Mr Stone then, nudging her urgently so that he could tell her how much he had enjoyed the duck.

Lady Forsyth didn't hold with modern music; after dinner they all repaired to the drawing room and sat about talking until she tapped Josephine on the shoulder and asked her to play for them all.

Josephine got up at once; she wasn't a conceited girl but she had a certain talent for the piano and went without fuss to the baby grand at the other end of the room and sat down.

'Something restful,' suggested the rector. He had a resonent voice very suited to the pulpit but rather loud in the drawing room.

'You please yourself, Jo,' said Lady Forsyth comfortably, 'I like it best when you ramble. . .'

So she rambled, going from Handel's *Water Music* to *Cats* and back to *Tales from the Vienna Woods* and then Chopin. After half an hour she stopped, sitting quietly with her hands in her lap while the company applauded and then with a wide smile and a quiet thank-you, slipping back to her chair by Wendy.

'It's not fair,' said Wendy cheerfully, 'you've more than your share of good looks, you've got a marvellous job and you can play the piano well enough to charm the birds off a tree.' She spoke without envy; even though Nicky Peacock, away on a business trip in America and whom she intended to marry, was tone deaf and disliked any kind of music; he didn't like career girls either, or dark hair. Wendy patted her blonde locks and nudged Josephine.

'I say, I like Julius, don't you? He's the right size for you too. . .' She gave a gasp, 'Oh, Jo, I'm sorry—Mother told me about Malcolm but I forgot. Do you feel awful about it?'

'Well, yes, I suppose I do, but I think I'm getting

over it. When's Nicky back?'

The pleasant evening ended and everyone began saying goodbye to everyone else. Mr Van Tacx was staying with the Forsyths, chatting idly to people as they went, but as Josephine followed her mother and father across the hall he wandered over to wish them good night.

'Half-past six tomorrow evening?' He asked Josephine.

Since her mother was standing right by them, she said politely, 'Thank-you, yes.'

They were barely in the car before Mrs Dowling asked, 'Is Julius taking you back, Jo?'

'Julius, so soon! Yes, Mother. He'll call for me at half-past six.'

There was a short silence, then, 'Church tomorrow,' observed Mrs Dowling, 'and the rector's preaching.' She sounded very satisfied about it.

Mr van Tacx arrived ten minutes early, to find Dr and Mrs Dowling sitting comfortably by the fire and no sign of Josephine.

'Out with Cuthbert,' volunteered Mrs Dowling. 'They miss each other dreadfully, you know. But she won't be far; she's quite ready, she told me so not an hour ago. If you like to go through the back door and shout she'll hear you; they'll be at the bottom of the orchard.'

Dr Dowling had cast down the Sunday papers he was reading when Mr van Tacx had followed Mrs Dowling into the room. 'My dear,' he said mildly, 'you can't expect Mr van Tacx to chase after Jo. . .'

Mr van Tacx exchanged a glance with Mrs Dowling. 'No, of course not,' said Mrs Dowling and smiled.

Josephine walking into the room at that moment, wondered why her mother looked so smug. She greeted the doctor pleasantly, observed that he was early, and went to get her coat and overnight bag.

She was vague as to when she would be home again, because Mr van Tacx was standing right by her and listening quite openly. 'I'll give you a ring.' She promised as she embraced her parents and got into the Bentley.

He had said that they would have a meal on the way. As they left Salisbury behind them, he said casually: 'I've booked a table at Sheriff House in Stockbridge. I hope you like it, perhaps you already know it?'

'I've not been there, Mother and Father have. They loved it.'

Presently he stopped the car and they went into the small hotel and Josephine, who hadn't been feeling in the least hungry, sniffed the fragrant faint smells coming from the kitchen as they crossed the hall, suddenly found her mouth watering.

They had a table by the window in the small dining room and she ate her way with wholesome appetite through homemade paté and toast, a morsel of trout, fresh caught from the river running through the hotel garden, followed by Tournedos Rossini and to round these off, an ice cream, home made, and as she explained to her companion, out of this world.

They drank hock sparingly since they still had more than an hour of their drive ahead of them but they didn't hurry over their coffee, and Josephine, almost against her will, found herself happy and content; Mr van Tacx was a pleasant companion, telling her a little of Holland although nothing of himself, not mentioning the hospital at all, never verging on the personal. It wasn't until he was turning into the hospital courtyard that she realised that she had told him a good deal more about herself and her family than she had ever meant to. As he brought the car to a halt she asked abruptly, 'What was she like? The girl you were going to marry?'

She wished the words unsaid as soon as they were out of her mouth, even though she waited for his answer.

'Now why do you want to know that?' He asked mildly. 'Can it be that you are a little interested in me after all?'

She undid her seat belt and put her hand on the door, but he stretched across her and put his own hand over hers so that she couldn't get at the lock. 'No, play fair, Josephine, you asked a question and I want to know why?'

'Curiosity. Idle curiosity. That's all.' Her voice had a decided snap.

'In that case I shan't bother to indulge it.' He got out of the car before she saw what he was doing, got her bag from the back and opened her door. 'A pleasant evening,' he commented blandly, staring at her.

'Yes, yes, it was. Thank you very much for bringing me back and for the gorgeous meal.'

'We shan't be seeing each other for a few days—Matt will take care of things until Thursday; I'll be back for the list.'

'Oh, you are going away?' She frowned, her tongue was running away with her again.

'Yes. Good night, Josephine.' He handed her her bag and stood watching her until she went through the door of the nurses home.

She went back to a busy ward in the morning; Mrs Prior wasn't so well; it seemed to Josephine that she wasn't making much effort to get better; true, the poor soul hadn't much of a future, but she didn't know that; her husband, truculent and apparently uncaring had been told that provided she responded to the radiotherapy, she would have several years still provided she could take things easily, but he had responded with a long self pitying tirade which had left Josephine worried. To send Mrs Prior home to someone who was obviously not going to bother about her wouldn't do at all. She mulled the situation over as she went about her work on the ward and found herself wishing that Mr van Tacx was there to sort the matter out for her.

She missed him; she told herself that it was his tiresome ways which she missed, knowing quite well that it wasn't anything of the sort; it was his reassuring person; his way, however annoying, of knowing exactly what to do; his ability to spur his patients on to greater efforts. She had seen how the ladies on the ward visibly relaxed when he came to do his round. By Wednesday evening she could hardly wait for Thursday; the theatre list was for the early afternoon, which meant that he would do a quick round before he went into theatre.

He was sitting at her desk when she went on duty in the morning, writing up charts and checking X-rays. He glanced up as she came to a halt in the doorway. 'Morning, Josephine. I'll be two minutes—you'll want to take the night report. I'll have Miss Potts up first—she's scared rigid, poor soul. And I want to talk to you about Mrs Prior when I've finished the list.'

He got up, leaving a fearful mess of papers on the desk. 'Nice to see you, Josephine—I missed you.' He reached the door and then turned round and bent to kiss her surprised mouth.

'Well,' said Josephine on a gusty breath, but he had already gone.

It was an effort to concentrate on the Night Nurse's report and presently when the night nurses had gone and she was going over the day's work with Joan, that young woman asked, 'Do you feel all right, Sister? You look—well a long way off.'

Josephine pulled herself together. 'I'm fine— just a bit worried about Mrs Prior and we are a nurse short, aren't we?'

She was off duty at five o'clock but the last case didn't come back from the recovery room until half an hour after that and it was another half hour before Mr van Tacx came to look at his patients. Josephine, tired by now and a little peevish, greeted him austerely, accompanied him to the various bedsides and handed him the charts to write up. He looked up when he had almost finished. 'You're off duty?'

'At five o'clock,' she said tartly.

He smiled faintly. 'And we still have to settle things for Mrs Prior. Had you a date for this evening?'

'No.' If she had been engaged to Malcolm still, she would have been hopping mad, now she was tired; once Mrs Prior's affairs had been settled all she wanted to do was to make a pot of tea and lie in a hot bath, and then bed, never mind about supper.

His eyes swept over her. 'You're tired.' He glanced at the thin gold watch on his wrist. 'I'll meet you in the hall in twenty minutes—we'll go to the Lion and the Lamb and eat a sandwich while we deal with Mrs Prior.'

'I—I was going to bed.'

'By all means, but after you've eaten.' He put down the charts and made for the door. 'Twenty minutes and don't bother to change.'

She couldn't be bothered to argue, let alone change; she went off duty after giving the report to Joan, washed her face and did her hair, flung on a tweed coat over her uniform dress and trailed down to the front hall. She felt despondent as well as tired; life stretched before her, empty at the moment—perhaps even Malcolm would have been better than the emptiness. She pulled herself up; it wasn't like her to be so full of self pity—

a holiday might be the answer—a week or two at home. She smiled at the thought and Mr van Tacx, watching her narrowly as she crossed the entrance hall, closed his eyes for a moment. When she looked up she saw him; his face was without expression, almost austere.

'I'm not very good company,' she warned him.

'That makes two of us.' He hurried her out of the courtyard and across the busy street and into the bar parlour of the pub, an establishment much patronised by the hospital medical and nursing staff. The stuffy little room was almost empty. Mr van Tacx sat her down at a corner table, said, 'I'll order for you, shall I?' and went over to the bar.

He came back shortly with a tankard of beer and a glass of something dark which he put down before her. 'Port,' he said, 'Just what you need. I've ordered some beef sandwiches.'

She took a sip from her glass and decided that it was rather nice. She had downed almost half of it by the time the sandwiches came and felt much better. She felt hungry too now, she took the sandwich he offered her and bit into it.

'You need a holiday,' said Mr van Tacx.

'Well, I was wondering if I'd have a week away.'

'At home?'

She nodded. 'It's my favourite time of the year. . .'

She gave a gasp when he asked abruptly, 'Where were you going for your honeymoon?'

She found herself answering meekly enough.

'Malcolm wanted to go to Spain—it's cheap there and warm of course. I—I didn't want to go there very much. They are not kind to their animals. . .'

He nodded. 'I know. Where did you want to go?'

'It's silly—just some small country hotel, in the Cotswolds or my own part of the country. . .'

'An excellent choice. Have another sandwich?' He smiled kindly at her and his eyes weren't cold any more. 'Do you feel able to cope with Mrs Prior's difficulties now?'

Of course that was why he had brought her here; she frowned a little; she had been chatting on about this and that and all the time he must have wanted to get down to the ward problems. 'Of course.'

'You know that she has a grandson she has never seen? Her daughter lives in Manchester.'

'Yes, she told me. Her husband says they can't afford to go there for a visit.'

'I've been in touch with a man I know; he'll get her into the radiotherapy hostel there; she could then have her treatment and be near her daughter. I'm willing to bet my last cent that she'll discover that life's worth living after all. We can spin out her convalescence and give her a month or two of happiness. I've arranged to see her husband tomorrow, I think it could be fixed up provided I can persuade him.'

The barman had brought cups of coffee and taken away their plates and glasses. Josephine sat looking at Mr van Tacx. 'That is a marvellous idea—you are sure that you can get him to agree?'

He looked at her with a faint smile. 'Quite sure, when will you take that holiday?'

'Well, not next week, the week after there'll be a Relief Sister free so I daresay I can get away then. I'll be back for Mr Bull. . .'

He said carelessly, 'So you will. . .'

'You'll go back to Holland?'

'Oh, yes. I have two partners, but I can't expect them to cope for too long.'

She longed to ask him where he lived at the same time reminding herself that she didn't care in the very least. She drank the last of her coffee and said rather primly, 'I'd like to go back, if you don't mind—it's been quite a busy day.'

He made no demur, which quite irrationally, annoyed her. And at the hospital entrance he opened the door for her, received her thanks with a casual nod and a pleasant good night, and turned on his heel and strode away. Josephine, feeling neglected, started to cross the entrance hall to be stopped by the porter on duty, holding out a letter for her.

'Came by the afternoon post, Sister, and got missed. Sorry.'

It was from Malcolm. She put it in her coat pocket and made her way to the Nurses Home, wondering what was inside. For two pins, she told herself crossly, if Malcolm wanted her to marry him after all, she would accept.

But Malcolm had no such desire; he wrote to ask if she would object to him selling the antique wall clock she had found in a dusty old shop and which they had bought together. The clock, he explained, was quite valuable and he would send her half of it's price when the deal was completed. She read the sparsely worded letter a second time, tore it into tiny pieces and went to run a bath. She lay in it for a long time, long after the water was disagreeably cool, weeping copiously.

CHAPTER FOUR

MR van Tacx was on the ward early the next morning, doing a very thorough round. At the end of it he dismissed the various people who had accompanied him, asked Matt if he would go and arrange for some X-Rays and followed Josephine into her office.

'And now what's the matter?' he wanted to know briskly. 'You've been crying—red nose, puffy eyes—where's your pride, girl?'

She rounded on him. 'Be quiet, do,' she snapped, 'and I would be obliged if you didn't poke your nose into my affairs. You have no right. . .'

He answered equably, 'No, I haven't, but I'm working on that.' His whole manner changed suddenly. 'I think that for your sake and that of your staff and patients you should arrange a holiday as soon as possible. You have a very able Staff Nurse who can no doubt manage the ward.'

She said coldly, 'Oh, yes—just as well as I can—probably better.'

'Now you are being foolish and that merely illustrates my point. You need a few days to pull yourself together—a blow to your heart and to your pride. You mentioned going away when the Relief Sister would be free, surely you can leave the ward to Joan for a few days before this Sister can take over? You need ten days at least.'

She was surprised at the upsurge of hurt feelings because he was so anxious to be rid of her; if she did as he suggested, there would be only a week at the outside before Mr Bull returned. She sat looking at her hands clasped tidily in her lap. He was right, of course; it had been a blow, more to her pride than her heart she admitted silently; she supposed that she had got into the habit of thinking that she was in love with Malcolm and now that they had parted she saw her mistake. All the same it had shaken her and it had been an effort to show her usual calm face to the world. She hadn't shown it to him though, had she? It was just bad luck that he seemed to come across her either in tears or mopping up after a howl.

The silence had gone on for rather a long while; she looked up and saw him watching her carefully. She said quietly, 'I'll arrange to go at the end of the week; it's my weekend anyway, I'll take a week's holiday and my days off added on to that—that's almost two weeks. There's only a short list next week because they're to put a new lamp in theatre and five patients are going home and there are only three to be admitted.'

Mr van Tacx, who knew all that already, nodded his handsome head. 'You dislike me very much at the moment,' he said blandly, 'but I assure you that it is for your own good that I make these suggestions.'

'Orders,' muttered Josephine under her breath, and then to make up for this piece of rudeness. 'Would you like coffee, sir?'

'In place of coals of fire, Josephine? Let us by all means bury the hatchet in the coffee pot.'

Her mouth, which never stayed anything but gentle for long; twitched into a smile. 'Where did you learn to speak English so very well?' she asked.

'I had a nanny. Indeed, she is still with us at my home. Elderly now of course, but very brisk and bossy. And then I was at Cambridge.'

She got up to go to the kitchen and ask for a coffee tray. With her hand on the door she observed thoughtfully, 'I suppose you're very clever.' She sighed without knowing it. 'I daresay you'll have quite a job finding a wife to please you.'

It was Mr van Tack's turn to smile. 'Ah, but I've found one who'll suit me very well, the question is will I please her?'

She decided not to answer that.

She had no trouble in getting a week's leave; the ward was ticking over nicely, Mrs Prior had, in some miraculous way, been fixed up at a Manchester Hospital; heaven knew what Mr van Tacx had said to her husband, but he had stumped into Josephine's office unannounced one evening and told her belligerently that he had agreed to let his wife go, adding nastily, 'She's not much use to me at 'ome, is she?'

'You will be able to visit her at weekends,' suggested Josephine coldly.

'Me? Go all the way up there? Not likely. I'll drop 'er a line.'

Josephine considered he would be no great loss

to his wife, indeed Mrs Prior's small pinched face glowed with happiness. Josephine, who could have started her leave on Friday evening, waited until Saturday morning so that she could see Mrs Prior on her way before getting into the Mini and taking herself off to Ridge Giffard.

It was a wet day, and cold, but driving along the lane to her home she couldn't have cared less. Two weeks, more or less, were hers in which to do exactly as she liked, and in that time, she had resolved, she would turn her back on the last few weeks; it was no good crying over spilt milk, and if the truth were told she knew now that it had been her pride which had suffered more than her heart; Mr van Tacx had hinted at that, hadn't he? and as he so often was, he was right.

She parked the Mini at the side of the house, collected her case and went in through the back door, to be greeted by her mother's wide smile and a lovely smell of something delicious cooking.

She slept dreamlessly that night and successive nights too, and the days, following a gentle pattern of chores around the house, walking a delighted Cuthbert, and driving her father on his rounds, slid together into a soothing whole. Of Malcolm she thought not at all and certainly she had no regrets now; with hindsight she realised that for the last few months she had been uneasy about getting married to him, she told her mother as much as they made beds together and the older woman said mildly, 'Yes, dear, we could see that. There's no one else?'

Josephine tucked in a corner. 'No,' and since

that didn't seem a very satisfactory answer: 'I hadn't fallen in love with anyone else, mother— that wasn't the reason we broke up. Perhaps I'll never marry now.'

'One never knows who is round the corner,' observed Mrs Dowling gently.

A remark Josephine remembered that afternoon as she plodded along with Cuthbert, both of them wet and enjoying it. There was a fierce wind soughing through the trees, cutting off other sounds, the Bentley, creeping up beside them sent Cuthbert into a crescendo of indignant barks and Josephine swinging round to meet Mr van Tacx's calm face, stuck out of the open window.

'Hullo,' he said, 'we seem fated to meet here, don't we? Having a pleasant walk?'

'Yes, thank-you.' She bent to hush Cuthbert, amazed to discover that she was pleased to see him. Her pleasure was short lived however.

'I need hardly ask if your holiday is doing you good; I can see that it is.'

He withdrew his head, waved a nonchalant hand, and drove on.

'Well, of all the rude men,' said Josephine, 'just let him wait until I see him again.' She marched home, her colour so high that her father, meeting her as she went indoors, remarked that he hadn't seen her look so fit for a long time.

Being a Saturday, the surgery was for urgent cases only so that her father was able to sit down to lunch at his leisure, and since it was still raining, once the washing up had been done, Josephine settled down to a game of bezique with him; it was pleasant in the sitting room with the flames from the log fire lighting the well polished furniture and the little reading lamp by her mother's chair casting a warm glow. She was, Josephine assured herself, more than content; it would have been nice if she could have seen Mr van Tacx just for a few minutes though, so that she could tell him just how ill mannered he was. Probably she would see him at church in the morning, but one could hardly haul him over the coals at the church door; besides the Branton House pew was on the other side of the church and its occupants always left first.

The weather had changed dramatically by the time she got up the next morning, the sun shone from a pale blue sky on to a world turned white by frost. Josephine, racing round the garden with Cuthbert found it exhilarating; she took him back to the kitchen where he settled down in front of the Aga with Mrs Whisker, and went upstairs to get ready for church. She emerged presently, looking quite delightful in her new tweed suit and severe matching felt hat perched at an angle, to drive her parents to church.

They were later than usual because Mrs Dowling had mislaid her spectacles and everyone had to search for them, and the church was already almost full. Doctor Dowling had had a pew at the front under the pulpit for years and they filed in. Josephine said her prayers rather hurriedly and sat back and presently turned her head just a trifle so that she could see the Branton House pew. Mr van Tacx was in it, towering over everyone else around him; his profile was all that she could see and very severe it looked too. She looked away, just too late, as he turned his head and saw her.

Leaving the church after the service was a slow business, her mother naturally knew everyone for miles around, and so did she and her father; progress to the porch was slow and then held up while they chatted to the rector. Mr van Tacx would be gone, in any case, it was hardly the place in which to pick a bone with him.

He wasn't gone, he appeared beside her, apparently out of thin air. His good morning included all three of them and Doctor and Mrs Dowling stopped to pass the time of day and then, after the doctor had received a speaking glance from his wife, wandered on, leaving Josephine with Mr van Tacx.

He wasted no time. 'A lovely day. If you're doing nothing for the rest of it, shall we go to Stourhead? I went last summer but I'm told that this is the time of the year when it is at its best.'

'Stourhead?' She stared at him. 'What about the Forsyths—I mean don't they expect you to stay—and be amused at Branton House?'

His firm mouth twitched. 'Er—I think I'd rather be amused in your company, besides they have a long standing engagement with some aunt or other and they will be glad if I can find something to do on my own.'

'Wendy. . .' began Josephine.

'A charming girl. I'll call for you in twenty minutes.' He glanced down at her elegant high heeled shoes. 'And wear a sensible pair of shoes,

I'd like to walk right round the lake.'

Josephine stood her ground. 'You were rather rude yesterday.'

He agreed gravely. 'You see, I hadn't expected to see you. I was thinking of you and then there you were.'

She decided to think that out later. 'Well, it's a nice day,' she smiled. 'I'll go and change my shoes.'

They parted, he to stride away between the tombstones towards the path leading to Branton House, she to get into the car with her patient parents. They agreed instantly that it was a lovely day and a shame to stay indoors, 'But don't forget that the park closes at dusk, though I suppose one could get out if one tried hard enough. I mean, go up to the house or go to the Spread Eagle.'

Josephine was ready and waiting, sensible lace up shoes on her feet, her face freshly made up, all the same she stayed in her room for a few minutes after he arrived; he was an arrogant man, she must remember to keep him in his place.

He made no effort to do anything but that; they drove through the country roads which would bring them to the A303. There was a little traffic only and they were turning into Stourton Village within a very short time, which had seemed even shorter because of the pleasant conversation they had enjoyed. There was no denying the fact that Mr van Tacx was an agreeable companion when he chose to be.

The Spread Eagle, on the edge of the park, was full of Sunday customers sitting around in the roomy bars, warmed by the great open fireplace with the roaring log fire. They found a table by a window and Josephine sipped sherry while her companion drank his beer. They ordered lunch while they sat and went through to the equally comfortable dining room to eat their roast beef and horseradish sauce and follow that with treacle tart and cream. They didn't linger over their meal; the walk round the lake would take them an hour or more and it was already getting on for two o'clock. They had coffee and set out. 'A pity there isn't time to look round the church,' said Josephine, 'it's rather nice.'

'Yes, I went round it briefly, but it deserves a long visit. We'll do that next time. Shall we go left or right?'

'Left,' said Josephine promptly, 'I like to save the grottos till last.'

The lake was on their right, the path wandering in and out of the trees beside it, sometimes right by the water's edge, sometimes almost out of sight. There were swans and ducks on the lake, most of them crowded on to the island close to the bridge they had just crossed.

It was quiet, everything still covered in a thin coating of frost, the firs rising to a great height all around them and the smaller trees still a colourful red and yellow, interspersed with masses of red berries. Their feet made no sound on the path and they didn't talk. All at once Josephine laid a hand on her companion's arm. 'A squirrel,' she said softly and they stood and watched the small creature until it raced up a tree. And when they walked on presently, she found her hand tucked under his arm. It would be ill mannered to remove it, she decided, and it was really quite delightful walking in the quiet beauty of the park; she hadn't felt so happy and content for days. She gave her head a metaphorical shake; it must be her surroundings which were making her sentimental. She asked briskly, 'Have you had a busy week?'

'Yes, but no busier than usual. I think. And you? what have you been doing with yourself?'

'Nothing—pottering round the house, cooking a bit, driving Father some of the time—going to the rectory for dinner one evening, going into Tisbury to shop, taking Cuthbert for walks.'

'You haven't missed St Michael's?'

'Not a bit. I love nursing and running a ward, I can't imagine doing anything else. But if I didn't have to work, I'd love to stay at home and just be a. . .' She paused, she had been going to say a housewife but she felt suddenly shy.

'Housewife?' asked Mr van Tacx. 'It's not supposed to be very fashionable nowadays, is it? But I imagine it to be twice as hard as an office job or a hospital job, for that matter. Cooking and running a house, bringing up the children, washing and ironing, pandering to a bad tempered husband when his day hasn't gone well.'

She stopped to look at him. 'My goodness, you do know a lot about it,' she observed.

'I hope to know more. Can I hear the waterfall? We must be quite near. . .'

They had got to the end of one side of the lake and started along the narrow path by the water at its head and presently they could see the waterfall, bright against the dark rock and trees surrounding it. The afternoon was fading, the sun a red ball turning the sky from blue to faint rosiness. They walked on, turning down the other side of the lake now, disgressing presently to peer into Diana's Temple, cold and sombre now as the sun was going down.

'It must have been rather fun,' observed Josphine, peering at the frescos round the walls, 'I mean, having got grottos and temples and gazebos all over the place; somewhere to walk each day. You wouldn't need to go out of the park at all.'

'Very romantic,' Mr van Tacx eyed the statues guarding the door, without much liking. 'Also damp. You would have to be very much in love too, sitting around on those stone benches in unsuitable clothing.'

Josephine chuckled. 'I don't believe you've an ounce of romance in you,' she declared and added hurriedly, 'I'm sorry—I shouldn't have said that—you must have, you were going to be married.'

They had left the temple behind them and taken a path between thick shrubs. 'The two aren't necessarily compatible. Where is this grotto?'

They went down some awkward steps to confront a small grotto with Neptune sitting in it. 'He looks cold,' said Josephine as they followed the narrow stone path and entered a series of grottos, very gloomy now in the half light, ornamented with statues at intervals and ending in a dark tunnel which brought them out by the lake once more.

Josephine shivered. 'I suppose they are at their best in the summer. All those stone statues. . .'

'Yes, personally I prefer flesh and blood. I find it hard to work up any romantic feelings over statues.'

'Perhaps we are not romantic anymore,' said Josephine wistfully, 'people had more time. . .'

'My dear girl, no one needs time to fall in love—one may not realise it when it happens, but sooner or later one becomes aware.'

'Just as one becomes aware that one has fallen out of love. . .' Josephine sounded wistful again.

'Quite so.' He sounded very casual. 'We're just in time I fancy. . .' He followed her through the gate. 'Would you like to have tea here?'

'I'm sure Mother will expect us—that is if you'd like to come?'

'Very much.' They drove back through the rapidly darkening evening, not talking much. He was, she had discovered, someone she could be with and not have to talk to all the time. This, she presumed, was what was meant by being at ease with someone. And yet they didn't really like each other. They had reached her home before she could give much thought to this and since Mrs Dowling had judged their return to a nicety and was on the point of making the tea, she had to shelve the problem.

They had tea round the fire in the drawing room; muffins dripping in butter, anchovy toast, delicately thin slices of bread and butter and one of Mrs Dowling's fruit cakes. Mr van Tacx ate everything offered him; their walk had given him an appetite, and as he pointed out to his hostess, he could think of nothing nicer than tea round the fire on a cold day.

'We don't have tea in Holland—at least, not all these delights—just tea—mostly without milk and a very small biscuit.' He sighed so loudly that Josephine gave him a suspicious look. 'I shall have to marry an English girl who is a good cook.'

'There must be plenty only too ready and willing,' said Mrs Dowling. A gentle, rather absentminded woman, she tended to say things which other people thought.

Mr van Tacx remained imperturbable. 'That is very kind of you to say so, Mrs Dowling, but I think that I would make a trying husband; I have a bad habit of speaking my mind and I like things my way—my wife would need to be a saint. . .'

'Or a girl who loves you.'

'That is probably more than I deserve.'

'Well, have another slice of cake,' begged Mrs Dowling comfortably.

It was after six o'clock when he got up to go. 'A delightful afternoon,' he observed, 'I shall remember it.' He spoke to Mrs Dowling and looked at Josephine. They were all standing in the hall and she had gone to open the door for him. He shook hands with her mother and father and he paused at the open door, bent his head and kissed her unhurriedly.

Josephine shut the door and listened to the gentle purr of the Bentley going away. There was a short silence before Mrs Dowling said happily, 'I've always liked the custom of social kissing, so civilised, if you know what I mean. The royal family always do. . .I find it very nice.'

Josephine found it nice too, though she didn't say so.

She was forced to admit by the middle of the week that she was looking forward to the weekend, just in case Mr van Tacx intended to spend it with the Forsyths, but Saturday came and went and there was no sign of him in church on Sunday. She told herself that it was really of no consequence; she had had a delightful week doing almost nothing and spending a good deal of time with Lucy and her various friends.

She had gone into Salisbury too and bought some clothes, a silky crepe dress in a dreamy green which she didn't really need at all, only it was so pretty, a jacket and skirt in what the sales lady described as bilberry and a couple of blouses and sweaters. She bought knitting wool too to make a chunky sweater in the Italian style and since she hadn't spent much on clothes for some time, a pair of ankle boots, strapped and buckled, which made her long legs look even longer.

'I'll leave the dress here, I think,' she told her Mother, 'It will do very nicely for the parties I might be home for round about Christmas.'

Her mother smoothed the soft fabric. 'It'll be no trouble to pack,' she observed, 'and it might come in handy—the odd evening out you know.'

She began to fold it away carefully into it's tissue paper. 'I am sure the young doctors ask you out, dear.'

'Yes, they do, but I don't always go, in fact I

haven't been out for ages, only with Malcolm.'

'Yes, well—he's not there anymore, is he? I should enjoy yourself, love, you are only young once.'

'And that's not going to last much longer.' Josephine was holding up one of the new blouses. 'Mother, supposing I don't marry. . .sometimes I wake up in the night and wonder whether I should have married Malcolm?'

'One has the silliest ideas in the middle of the night, dear. I can't think why. You know quite well that you wouldn't have been happy with Malcolm, and I'm quite sure that you'll marry.' She paused, 'Quite sure.'

Josephine leaned over and kissed her mother. 'What a comfort you are. If I come home on my next days off shall I see Mike and Natalie?'

'They'll be here, let me see—in two weeks time—just for the weekend, but they will be home for Christmas. Will you be able to get off this year?'

'Perhaps for a day—I'll have to be there for Christmas Day; I'll try for Christmas Eve.'

She parked the Mini in its usual place, trying not to notice the petrol laden air and the damp faintly foggy atmosphere. St Michael's loomed behind her, looking particularly Victorian, she walked round to the front entrance to collect any post there might have been for her while she had been away and that was only a shade better, although with all its ornamental stonework and unnecessary wrought iron embellishments, it was an improvement on the new wing. She went inside, collected her letters, wished the porter on duty a good evening and went across to the nurses' home. She was on duty the next morning and she had her uniform to get ready and a cap to make up which she did while she caught up with the hospital news.

Supper was over, her friends were going to and fro along the sister's corridor, intent on hot baths, cups of tea, and in a few cases, getting changed to go out for the evening. They popped in and out of her room as they went, pleased to see her back, throwing titbits of news at her. Mercy had got engaged, Caroline had bought a new outfit and Moira Carson—she surely knew the Staff Nurse in the recovery room—was making a play for Mr van Tacx.

Josephine put down her mug of tea; Moira was a redhead, small and slender and very sexy—not at all the sort of girl she would have chosen for Mr van Tacx. He was, of course old and wise enough to choose anyone he fancied and really she couldn't care less if he was fool enough to fall for Moira; everyone knew that she was out to catch a husband, preferably one with well lined pockets. Mr van Tacx undoubtedly had those and the good looks and elegant appearance as an added bonus. Apparently he hadn't the wit to see through Moira's wiles.

'Good luck to him,' she said so sharply that her companions looked at her in surprise, and then changed the conversation rapidly. Poor old Jo—still smarting from her broken engagement.

It took all her willpower to shut the little episode

out of her mind once she was in bed. She assured
herself that she didn't like him, well she liked him
better than she had done at first, but not enough
to mind about Moira. He had been kind about her
breakup with Malcolm, probably he thought that
she had quite recovered from that and he need not
act the friend any more, and Moira, rather disliked
by her colleagues, could turn on the charm if she
thought it worth her while.

Josephine thumped her pillows and closed her
eyes firmly. It was none of her business. She
turned her thoughts to the morrow's work; quite
a task for she kept remembering Stourhead. It
struck her forcibly that just for a time, while they
had been there, she had been really happy.

There was no trace of the light hearted woman
who had shared his walk there when she met him
the following morning. She had already done her
own round and studied the charts, the ward was
exactly as she liked it to be; she met him at the
door with her usual calm.

Matt was with him as well as a handful of students and a very new houseman. She greeted them
politely and led the way to the first bed. By the
time they were half way round the ward she had
decided that her idea that this friendship had been
merely transitory had been a sound one. He was
friendly still but in an austere manner which took
all the warmth from it. He took his time over his
patients, making time to talk to each of them,
explain what he intended doing and why, giving
her instructions as they went and finally, when the
round was finished, sitting at her desk in the office,

writing up the charts, conferring with Matt, taking care that the new houseman should have a chance to give an opinion.

Josephine served the coffee, gave answer to any questions put to her, and passed the biscuits. They all left presently and from his manner Mr van Tacx might have just met her for the first time.

It was at dinner that Caroline, arriving late, passed on the interesting bit of news that Moira had got a date with Mr van Tacx that evening.

'And I'm sure she deserves it,' said Caroline, 'she's worked hard enough for it.'

Josephine eyed her plate of wholesome shepherd's pie; she had no appetite.

'A flash in the pan?' asked someone.

'You know our Moira—once she's got a toe in the door. . .' Several pairs of eyes were turned on to Josephine. 'Jo—you see him several times a week. What do you think? Is he going to hold out against that girl's wiles?'

'She's very pretty,' said Josephine, always a fairminded girl. 'And she's small and—and help-less—I daresay he might like that; he's so large.'

Aware of her own splendid proportions, she wished that she might be small and fairylike and be able to look wistful. Quite beyond her; all she could do was cry her eyes out at the wrong moments.

It was the following day, again at dinner, when she was told the details. She had gone down late because one of the patients had taken a bad turn and she had had to get Matt and set up a drip, and only Caroline was still at the table. She was picking her way daintily through rice pudding and stewed apple.

Josephine fetched cold meat, beetroot and potatoes and sat down opposite her. 'Busy morning?' she asked.

Caroline abandoned her pudding. 'So-so. Dentals and a couple of emergencies. A good thing it wasn't Mr van Tacx's list.'

'Why?'

Caroline giggled. 'Moira's spitting fire this morning. Oh, she had her evening out with Mr van Tacx, she also had an evening out with Sister Clark. . .' She paused for effect; Sister Clark was in her fifties, cosily plump and with no looks to speak of. 'And just by way of making a fourth, there was Mr Dean.' Mr Dean was the Senior Pharmacist, elderly, a little hard of hearing and an expert on the growing of roses.

Josephine put down her knife and fork. 'Go on,' she begged.

'They had a smashing meal at some posh restaurant, nothing spared,' she paused to laugh. 'Moira told me that the talk was of roses and Sister Clark's retirement and where she should retire to, beyond a few polite nothings at the beginning and end of the evening she didn't exchange a word with Mr van Tacx. She says she'd rather die than go out with him again. But he won't ask her; he's deep that man.'

Josephine agreed silently. The day which had so far been extremely tiresome, all at once became quite bearable.

She had handed over to Joan for the evening

and was sitting at her desk tidying away the papers on it when Mr van Tracx walked in. She put down the diet sheets she was holding and asked: 'You wanted to see someone, sir?'

'Yes, you. You're off duty?' He didn't wait for her to answer. 'So am I for an hour or so. Shall we go out to dinner?'

She sat looking at him. 'Who with?' she asked innocently.

He let out a great crack of laughter. 'The grape vine. Shall I say that I believe in safety in numbers?' He sat down on the edge of the desk. 'No one else—just us.'

'But then there's no safety. . .'

'Ah, there you are wrong, Josephine. I always feel safe with you.'

The kind of quenching remark that he was so good at making.

'In that case. . .thank you, yes I should like to come out this evening.'

'Half-past seven at the entrance. We'll go to the Savoy and dance.'

An excellent opportunity to wear the new green crêpe. Josephine lost no time in going to her room and preparing for the evening.

The Bentley was outside the entrance as she reached the hall and Mr van Tacx was leaning against a wall talking to the Senior Anaesthetist. He was wearing a black tie and she was profoundly glad that she had worn the green crêpe, anything less wouldn't have done justice to his elegant appearance.

He had seen her without appearing to look up,

for he nodded to his companion and crossed the entrance hall to meet her.

'Oh, very nice,' he told her, studying her person. The dress was simple, without fuss or frills, cut low, but not too low, and it fitted perfectly. Josephine, nice girl though she was, had made it her business to find out what Moira had worn— white chiffon with a great cluster of silk roses and a positively indecent front only partly veiled by a vulgar necklace of rhinestones. Josephine, playing safe, had no jewellery at all.

He took her to the Savoy; she hadn't been before and she found it impressive. They had a table in what she realised was a very good position and the restaurant manager greeted them as though he knew Mr van Tracx well. She sat down composedly, accepted a glass of sherry and per-used the menu. She chose salmon mousse, tournedos sauté with straw potatoes and baby sprouts and on being asked if she would like to dance, got up at once.

Their steps suited very nicely and being a tall girl, they were able to hold a conversation without suffering a crick in the neck. They went back to their table presently and then danced again before Josephine, with a fine disregard for calories, chose sherry trifle for afters.

The evening, made even more pleasant by the champagne they were drinking, went too swiftly; they sat over their coffee, talking with the ease of old friends, and then danced again until Josephine enquired about the time.

'Just gone midnight.'

'My goodness—I had no idea. There's a list in the morning and admissions.'

'All of which you will deal with without fuss or flurry. What are you worrying about, Josephine?'

'I'm not worried, it's just that I remembered suddenly. I'd forgotten everything. . .'

'Now that is a nice thing to say; I take it that you are enjoying your evening?'

'Oh, I am, I am. I can't remember when I've had such a super time.'

'Not even with Malcolm?'

She gave him a level look. 'Not even with Malcolm, Mr van Tacx.'

'Do you suppose you might call me Julius? I may be older than you, Josephine, but do you need to emphasise it?'

'But I can't—I mean you're a consultant. . .'

'Oh, we'll mind our manners on the ward; I thought I'd been doing rather well although it would be difficult to be otherwise when you confront me with a face as starched as your apron.'

She laughed then. 'Its absurd really, we don't even like each other do we? and yet we get on so well.' She paused, 'Although I must say that you annoy me very much indeed sometimes.'

He raised his eyebrows. 'And I try so hard to be a model of politeness.'

'Yes, and you are being amused behind it. Besides, you. . .sometimes you behave as though you can't get away fast enough.'

'To which I have no answer! Shall we dance just once more?'

A most unsatisfactory reply, but she had asked

for the snub. Probably tomorrow he would look at her with cold eyes—she would have to cultivate a frosty manner to match that.

He wished her a pleasant good night, assured her that he had enjoyed the evening even more than she had and begged her not to thank him, then saw her safely into the entrance hall before getting back into his car. She wondered as she went along to her room, what his flat near Harrods was like. And for that matter, where he lived when he went back to Holland. She frowned at the thought; Mr Bull would be back very soon now and Mr van Tacx would go away. 'And I shall forget him in no time at all,' she assured herself in a firm voice as she got into bed. She was tired out after a day's work and a night's dancing, she was asleep within minutes.

CHAPTER FIVE

THE morning brought its usual routine, women, anxious and trying to hide it, to be prepared for theatre, and more women, just as anxious, to be admitted. Josephine went from one to the other, reassuring in a soothing voice while she slid the pre-op injection into timid arms and then went to receive equally timid new patients, accompanied by even more timid husbands. Even after several years she felt for them; what to her was a commonplace operation with almost no risk attached to it was a gigantic upheaval for the patient and her family. She smoothed the way with cups of tea and sympathy and sensible advice and in between that went with the operation cases for that day to theatre, holding a trembling hand in her own gentle one and talking quietly about mundane things, so that the patient, already half asleep from her premed; took comfort from the fact that the world around her was just as it always was.

It was impossible to go to her midday dinner; she hastily ate a sandwich in her office and drank the strong tea Mrs Cross had made for her, and then went back to the ward to spend some time supervising the return of yet another patient from theatre.

Mr van Tacx came during the afternoon, breathing confidence into the new patients, causing the convalescent ladies to sit up and comb their hair surrepticiously, and carefully examining the operation cases. They were all straightforward and once they had wakened thoroughly, had a few sips of tea, another injection and their own nighties put on for them they settled down to another sleep. He went quietly from bed to bed with Josephine and Matt, giving low voiced instructions, scribbling in his atrocious writing on the charts Josephine had ready and then bidding her a courteous good afternoon; and she, longing for her tea, replying just as courteous. Where, she wondered, was the man she had danced with for hours on the previous evening? She gave him a frowning look and met his eyes, chilly and enquiring under raised brows. She blushed faintly, at the same time managing to look very severe. Mr van Tacx, making a leisurely exit, was amused.

Mr Bull was due back in two days time but Mr van Tacx had given no hint as to when he was leaving. Josephine found herself wondering more and more about this and if a suitable occasion had presented itself she would have asked him. But it didn't, the two days passed with only the minimum conversation between them, and that concerning the patients. On the third day Mr Bull came steaming on to the ward, driving an unhappy contingent of students before him. Of Mr van Tacx there was no sign.

Josephine led the way from bed to bed and Mr Bull hummed and hawed, firing questions at the hapless students, leaving the patients' notes scattered all over the place as he progressed. But presently he had done and she guided him to the office while the students, told to make themselves scarce, did so without a second bidding.

Over coffee he discussed the patients at some length and presently said, 'Mr van Tacx and I have gone over each case together, of course. He seems to have got through an unconscionable amount of work. He's a splendid surgeon but drives himself too hard.'

He glanced at Josephine as he spoke, she didn't say anything, but when he added, 'Pays me the compliment of doing exactly as I would do, too. . .'

She said quietly. 'We all found Mr van Tacx pleasant to work with, sir.'

'Yes, yes, I'm sure. He's a good chap—very old friend of mine. A pity he's gone back to Holland.'

'Oh!' said Josephine faintly, 'Has he? For good? He didn't say.'

'Oh, he'll be back,' declared Mr Bull tantalizingly. And with that she had to be content.

But there was no sign of him; a week passed and Mr Bull had no more to say on the subject. Josephine found herself wondering where Mr van Tacx was and what he was doing and the more she told herself sternly that it was of no interest to her the more she was wondering.

She found her usual calm disposition severely tried; the patients were tiresome even though she didn't allow them to know that, and the nurses were the worst in the hospital. She took herself off to go home for her free weekend with guilty relief.

She drove home through a nasty cold evening with the threat of frost and icy roads later. Perhaps once she was home she would be able to shake off the peevishness and the sense of emptiness about the future. She was tired, she told herself, as she turned thankfully into the gates of her home. Supper and bed and a good night's sleep and she would feel herself in the morning. She got out of the car into the teeth of a biting wind and found herself wondering if the wind was blowing in whichever part of Holland Mr van Taxc lived.

Probably it was, only he wasn't there. He was sitting opposite her father in the sitting room, enjoying a learned discussion concerning the modern technique in anaesthesia. Josephine, having greeting her mother in the kitchen, paused in the sitting room door to gape at him.

'Well,' she said on a long drawn out breath, 'Well—Mr Bull said you were in Holland,' and she remembered to kiss her father and mutter a greeting, and added belatedly, 'Good evening, Mr van Tacx.'

He got to his feet, towering over her although she was a big girl. 'You know, I do love to give these little surprises from time to time,' he observed mildly, 'and why am I Mr van Tacx? What have I done that I am no longer Julius?'

Josephine pinkened and bit her lip. She cast an exasperated look at her father. 'You took me by surprise,' she said slowly. She felt the pink deepen to red when he said cheerfully, 'Oh, dear, have you forgotten me already?'

Josephine answered clearly and not truthfully: 'I have had no occasion to think of you. . .'

'Not even to wonder where I had got to?' He

was smiling at her in a most beguiling manner.

She found it hard to fib under that blue gaze. 'Well, I suppose I did—just now and then.' She became all at once very polite:

'Are you staying at Branton House?'

'For the weekend, yes. Your Mother has kindly invited me to remain to supper.'

Dr Dowling got up. 'Ah, yes—just time for a drink. Run up to your room, Jo, and take off your things and fetch your mother in for a glass of sherry.'

Josephine went meekly away, her feelings so mixed that she didn't allow herself to think while she tidied herself and then went back to the kitchen.

'Steak and kidney pudding,' observed Mrs Dowling, stirring something in a saucepan, 'sprouts and artichokes and I'll cream the potatoes, and there is a mince tart and cream for afters.' She was a splendid cook. She added, 'a good wholesome meal cooked properly, I hope Julius likes plain food.'

'He will if you've cooked it,' Josephine assured her mother, 'you know you are a marvellous cook.' She took off her mother's apron. 'Father's waiting to hand round the sherry.'

Mr van Tacx appeared to be enjoying himself, but there was no telling what he was thinking behind that controlled face, Josephine decided. He ate a splendid supper, complimenting her mother's cooking with just the right degree of flattery, engaging in another discussion with her father on the subject of rose growing and excepting when good manners made it necessary, ignored her. So it was all the more surprising when, after the meal while they were drinking their coffee in the sitting room he should fix her with a compelling eye and suggest that they might go for a walk the following morning.

'Oh, I couldn't possibly,' she told him, too quickly, 'I've several things I must do. . .'

'Then after lunch. It seems unlikely to rain and I'm sure you don't mind a strong wind,' he went on unforgivably, 'it will blow away your peevishness.'

'My. . .well. . .' Her splendid bosom heaved with strong feelings and then hardly knowing why she did, she smiled. 'You're quite right. I'll bring Cuthbert.'

'Good.' He looked at Mrs Dowling who had been listening avidly. 'May I drive over and leave the car here? About two o'clock? That will give us two hours of daylight.'

'Of course you can, Julius. You'll stay to tea, won't you?'

'If I may.' He could charm the birds off a tree, decided Josephine, watching him. But not, she told herself firmly, me.

All the same she was ready when he arrived the next afternoon, well wrapped against the wind. But the day was bright and there had been a frost during the night, only the low bank of heavy cloud beyond the hills gave warning that the rain wasn't far off. With luck they would be home before it started.

Both the doctor and his wife saw them off; it

was her father's free weekend although he had taken surgery that morning, now he stood with her mother in the roomy old porch, comfortable in his slippers, a newspaper under his arm, the prospect of a couple of hours by the fire before him. He watched the pair of them turn into the lane beyond the short drive before closing the door. 'They make a good pair,' he observed to his wife.

Mrs Dowling led the way to the sitting room. 'Yes, dear. Someone told me—oh, up at Branton House, that he was engaged to be married but it seems the whole thing was called off. Poor man.'

The Doctor shook out his paper. 'I imagine that Julius is quite capable of managing his own life.'

'Yes, dear,' Mrs Dowling was all meekness. 'Just like our Jo.'

The lane was a nasty mixture of frozen mud and ruts, neither of which bothered Josephine or her companion, walking briskly away from the house and the village with Cuthbert between them.

'You have a walk in mind?' asked Mr van Tacx.

'If you don't mind rough ground—we can go over the stile into Pake's field and cross Stoney Bottom and come out into Paul's Marsh, that will bring us out on the other side of the village. It's about six miles.'

They walked in a companionable silence, exchanging the odd remark from time to time. Pake's field was sown with winter wheat faintly green in the hard ground, and they kept to the hedges with Cuthbert, a country bred dog who knew better than to cross a field until he was told

he might, at their heels. But Stoney Bottom was
at different matter—a wild stretch; its stones
hidden by shrubs and undergrowth and hummocks
of coarse grass and puddles of frozen water. The
frost was still heavy on the bushes and undergrowth and the watery sun gave the sombre place
unexpected beauty. There were birds too, black-
birds and a robin or two, starlings in plenty and a
wren, peering from the tangle of Old Man's beard
woven between the willows and the oak trees,
small and stunted and old, growing miraculously
in the poor soil. Josephine stopped when they were
half way across and emptied her pockets of the
bread she had brought with her, and they stood
and watched the hungry birds feeding.

'It isn't really a marsh,' explained Josephine as
they climbed the rather rickety gate beyond the
trees, 'it gets waterlogged if it rains a great deal,
otherwise the paths aren't too bad.'

'Only muddy,' observed Mr van Tacx, looking
down at his once beautifully polished brogues.

'You don't mind? We're used to muddy boots in
the winter but of course if you live in London. . .'

He turned to look at her. 'I don't. I live in
Holland, on the edge of a small village with more
than its share of mud in the winter.'

'You're going back to Holland?'

'Very shortly, yes.' He smiled faintly and she
went a little pink because she had been fishing
and he knew it.

There was quite a lot of Paul's Marsh, and by
the time they had reached the other side and the
village was in sight once more the sky had dark-

ened, and as they passed the first row of cottages it began to rain. As they went up the drive to the back door, Josephine thought how cosy her home looked with the downstairs windows lighted and the curtains undrawn. They left their things in the small stone lobby and Mr van Tacx offered to dry off Cuthbert while Josephine went to help her mother carry in the tea tray. 'Come straight through when you're ready,' she called to him as she picked up the tea tray and presently the pair of them followed her, Mr van Tacx to settle himself by the fire and Cuthbert to most firmly nose the cat to one side so that he might have the lion's share of the warmth.

They had polished off the crumpets and anchovy toast and Mrs Dowling was cutting the chocolate cake when the 'phone rang.

'I'll get it,' said Josephine and uncurled herself from the cushion in front of the fire. She was back very quickly, 'Father, there's been an accident out at Burke's farm; a pile up outside the yard gate—a milk tanker, a furniture van and he thinks two cars, and there is a tree blown down at the end of the lane. . .'

Her father said quickly, 'So an ambulance and the police can't get through. He was already on his feet and so was Mr van Tacx. 'I'll speak to Burke—get my bag Jo, and you'd better wear your boots.'

Mr van Tacx followed her into the lobby. 'If there are some boots to fit me?' he asked.

'Father's new ones—they're too big for him and he's not much smaller than you.' She added unnecessarily, 'You're coming too?'

'If I may. I'll turn the car, shall I? Give me that bag. . .'

'I'd better get the splints and slings.' She cocked her pretty head to listen. 'Father's 'phoning the police.'

He was with them a few moments later, calling to his wife to ring Dr Wells and Dr Jenkins in neighbouring villages; they were in the car and driving through the heavy rain seconds after that.

Burke's farm was almost three miles outside the village, deep in the countryside at the end of a long winding lane. Mr van Tacx turned the Bentley off the road, going slowly now and a good thing too, for a couple of hundred yards up the lane the tree, an old elm, had blocked the way completely. Mr van Tacx muttered something forceful and foreign under his breath and backed the car carefully. He had been travelling slowly enough to notice a gate on his right and stopped obediently at Josephine's crisp, 'That's right, stop a minute, I'll get the gate open—it's a nursery field for calves and cows and there won't be anything in it now; you can park the car inside and I'll shut the gate.'

She shivered as she got out of the car, the rain was icy now and the ground hard beneath her boots. Mr van Tacx parked his car with the efficiency she would have expected of him and he and her father got out.

They could see the farm now, for Mr Burke had had the sense to turn on every light in the place so that Mr van Tacx's powerful torch wasn't really needed as they hurried towards it, keeping to the hedge. There was a gate at the end of the field and they paused for a moment to take in the utter confusion on the other side of it. The milk tanker had jack-knifed as it was leaving the farm yard, hitting a furniture van, the contents of which were strewn in every direction, drowned in the milk pouring from a great gash in the tanker's side, but worse than that, caught between these two was a small car, hopelessly entangled. Mr Burke was there and two of his farm hands, struggling to free the tanker driver, trapped behind his wheel. There was a man sitting by the side of the lane, his head in his hands, and somewhere a woman was screaming in high pitched terror.

'Get that man indoors,' said Dr Dowling, 'and come back as quickly as you can.' He shouted at Mr Burke, 'Is your wife home, Burke?'

'Out, thank God,' bawled the farmer, 'taken the kids to Tisbury.'

Josephine didn't wait to hear any more, she heaved the man to his feet and looked him over; he wasn't injured, but shocked, She hauled him into the farm kitchen, poured him a cup of tea providentially brewing on the stove, found a blanket and laid him down on the shabby roomy sofa against the wall.

'You're quite safe,' she told him soothingly, 'just stay there. I'll be back in a minute or two. Close your eyes if you can and doze. Everything's all right.'

Far from all right she discovered when she went back into the yard. The tanker driver was still in his cab and her father was bending over him. Mr van Tacx had compressed his vast person into a tiny space in a tangle of metal which had been a car; his head and most of his shoulders had been thrust through a side window and he was pulling gently at something inside. Josephine picked her way carefully as near as she could get to him. 'Can I help?'

'Catch hold,' he told her and carefully drew a toddler through the broken window, 'indoors as fast as you can, take a quick look and do what you can, then get back here.'

The child was conscious, indeed as she entered the house it opened it's eyes and gave a healthy howl, much to her relief. In the kitchen she laid her gently on the table and examined its small arms and legs carefully, and then it's chubby body and head. She could find no injury other than a few scratches and the child, a bonny girl, was crying now in a satisfyingly normal way. The man was sitting on the sofa now, looking a better colour, Josephine picked up the child and set her on his knee. 'Cuddle her,' she urged him, 'she's frightened but I don't think she is hurt, keep her warm, and talk to her.'

He nodded, not quite himself yet, but he was all that was available. She flew out into the yard again, just in time to hear Mr van Tacx's calm voice saying: 'Come on girl,' and when she said, 'I'm here,' he passed another small child to her. This one was silent. 'Head injuries I think. Cope as best you can; Mother and Father are still here but I don't think I can get them out without some lifting gear.'

His voice sounded oddly dim from inside the car, it also sounded calm and matter-of-fact. She caught a glimpse of the two crumpled figures by the light of his torch before she turned and made her careful way back to the house.

Another little girl, older than the first, unconscious but breathing well despite the nasty gash on her head. Josephine put her on the table, fetched water from the sink and cleaned the cut and then went carefully over the small body, looking for injuries. A broken arm, some nasty abrasions on both legs and a hefty bump on the opposite side to the gash. But the pupil reactions were normal and the child's colour was fairly good. Josephine found a thick plaid cape hanging behind the door, wrapped the child carefully in it and asked the shocked man, 'Do you think you could manage to keep an eye on her as well? She's had a knock on the head and there's a broken arm, but if I lie her down beside you, perhaps you could keep her safe? It won't be much longer now.'

The man nodded. He was a better colour now and his eyes had come alive. She poured him some more tea, patted his shoulder and with a quick 'bless you,' left him. Not an ideal arrangement, she had to admit but there might be something she could do in the yard.

The police had arrived; two stalwart men, and since it was impossible to do more for the three unconscious people trapped, they set about clearing the approach to the yard so that when the

ambulance men and the firemen arrived they
would be able to move more freely. The milk was
almost ankle deep in the road by now and some
of the household possessions were shifting around,
banging into the roadside walls and each other. Dr
Dowling went to look at the children and Mr van
Tacx was heaving tables and chairs through the
open gate into the field. They had cleared a path
at least by the time the firemen with their cutting
equipment arrived and Josephine, at a word from
her father, went back to the kitchen while he and
Mr van Tacx gathered round the man in the cab
as the men set to work to free him.

Her patients kept her busy; the older of the two
little girls was still unconscious, the younger child
was wailing unhappily and the man had fallen into
an uneasy doze. He woke as she picked up the
toddler and complained that he felt sick, and by
the time she had the pair of them more comfortable
and had checked the younger child half an hour
had gone by. Still cuddling the little girl she went
to the door and looked out. The driver of the tanker
was being carried away on a stretcher and more
ambulance men were waiting to receive the two
limp forms being taken oh so slowly from the
tangled mass of their car. Someone had rigged
up a floodlight and the scene looked nightmarish
although none of the men working so feverishly
there looked other than calm, and when they spoke
it was in normal voices with no sign of panic. And
yet, she thought with suddenly awakened horror,
fire could have broken out at any moment while
they were at their work. The man and woman were

carried carefully away, her father going with them, and one of the policemen came into the kitchen to tell her that they would take the man to hospital in their car. 'There's an ambulance man coming for the children now,' he explained, 'the doctor wants to take a look at them first, though. A couple of our men will be here for a while yet. Is there someone to take you back, Miss?'

'I'll take her with me,' said Mr van Tacx from the door. 'Shall I take a quick look at the children? Dr Dowling asked me to check them before they go?' He looked at Josephine. 'Anything worrying you about them?'

She shook her head. 'This one,' she glanced down at the now sleeping child in her arms, 'is just scared and hungry and wants her mother, the other one is still unconscious but her pulse isn't too bad and her colour is better. Father thought her badly concussed but said she was to be treated as a fractured skull until she's been X-rayed.'

Mr van Tacx nodded and went to where the child lay. Presently he straightened up. 'She's fit to be moved. I suggest they are carried in blankets to the ambulance.' He smiled across at the police officer. 'You are seeing to this man? Taking them to Salisbury I expect. Odstock, isn't it? If you should want me you can reach me through Dr Dowling or at St Michael's in London.'

It took only a short time to see the children safely on their way, each carried by an ambulance man and once the van driver had been escorted away by a kindly policeman they were left in a suddenly quiet kitchen. Mr Burke and his men were still in the yard, helping to disentangle the bits and pieces locked so firmly together. At least the milk had stopped pouring over everything and what furniture could be saved had been piled on one side and in the field. She stood beside Mr van Tacx at the open door watching.

'They've started to clear the tree,' he told her. 'Once they can get up the lane they can have the tanker towed away.' He looked down at her; she was tired and grubby, her face streaked with dust, her hair hanging in a tangle and she stared back crossly, expecting him to make some nasty remark about her. He looked the worse for wear himself, anyway. He was weary for a start and it showed in his face, his hair was grey with dust and his car coat had got torn. He smiled suddenly and warmly. 'We make a fine pair,' he observed. 'I don't think they need us anymore, I'll take you home. Your father said he'd get a lift back with the Tisbury ambulance. Perhaps I might be allowed to ring the hospital and see how things are?'

'Yes of course. The man and woman—they're badly hurt?'

'Yes, but not, I think, fatally. Let's say goodbye to Mr Burke.'

They spent a few minutes with the farmer, feeling relieved to see that more men had arrived to help him. 'We'll 'ave 'em all settled 'fore no time,' he assured them, 'and thankee kindly, the pair of you, Miss Jo and you, sir. It'll not be forgotten, not for many a day.'

'Your wife and children? Do you want them

fetched or can you make some arrangement for them?'

'I jes' 'phoned: They'll stay in Tisbury and come 'ome in the morning.' Mr Burke put out a hamlike hand and engulfed first Jo's and then Mr van Tacx's hands in a bone crushing grip. 'A nasty old day, but we've come through it, eh? That tree'll be gone by morning and let's 'ope the poor souls is better.'

Mr van Tacx took her arm as they made their way through the field, back to the car at it's end. Mr van Tacx popped her into the front seat and went to open the gate, drove neatly out into the lane, shut the gate and got in beside her again.

It was still raining but not very hard any more; Josephine sat half asleep beside him and was glad that he didn't talk. The car slid to a smooth halt outside the house and her mother flung open the door at once.

'Come on in—Julius, you too. . . Jo. You're all right? Your father just 'phoned from Odstock. . .'

She took their coats, offered slippers as they kicked off their boots and led the way into the kitchen. 'Soup,' she said, 'and Julius, go along to the drawing room and get yourself a whisky and bring sherry for Jo will you? You know where you can clean yourself up. Jo, go and wash, love, and come back here.'

They did as they were told because they were too tired to do anything else and presently they were back in the warm kitchen, sitting at the table with bowls of soup in front of them while they had their drinks and Mrs Dowling buttered toast.

She let Mr van Tacx have his whisky before she said, 'Could you possibly drive into Salisbury, Julius, and collect my husband? The ambulance from Tisbury has been called out again—he thought he'd be another half hour or so. Could you ring the hospital when you've had that soup?'

This was a man she hadn't really known, Josephine reflected as she spooned her soup; a kind man, not in the least arrogant either, cheerfully agreeing to fetch her father although probably his plans for the evening had been completely spoiled. Who knew, perhaps he had been going out to dinner with some girl or other, even if he had planned to dine at the Forsyths, it wouldn't have been soup and toast and a great pot of tea to follow the whisky. At any rate he was enjoying the soup, she thought, watching her mother give him a second helping.

'What's the time?' she asked suddenly.

'Nine o'clock.'

'It can't be—we were having tea...'

'A lot has happened since then,' he told her gravely.

Curiosity got the better of her. 'Your evening is spoilt. Had—had you planned anything?'

He smiled at her and annoyed her very much by not answering her but turned to Mrs Dowling instead. 'Did you 'phone the Forsyths, Mrs Dowling? They knew I was here...'

'Oh, yes. They said not to worry and to join them when you were able and if you were too late or tired, they'd quite understand. I should have told you sooner, but I was so glad to see you both back. . .'

'Of course. If you'll excuse me, I'll fetch Dr Dowling. If I might 'phone the hospital?'

He had gone within ten minutes and Josephine helped her mother clear away and wash up and put things ready in case her father needed a meal when he got back.

'Have your bath and get ready for bed, darling,' counselled Mrs Dowling, 'I expect Julius will drop your father off on his way back to the Forsyths. What a mercy it's Sunday tomorrow and your father is free.'

Josephine did as she had been told; she was tired and grubby and she would have to wash her hair. She had a bath and with her bright hair hanging down her back, went downstairs. Her father would have news of the injured, especially of the children and she knew that she wouldn't sleep until she found out if they were going to recover.

The kitchen door was shut and she could hear the murmur of voices; her father was back. She opened the door and went in.

Mr van Tacx was back too, sitting at the table with a mug of coffee before him, talking quietly to her mother and father.

Josephine stopped short. 'Oh, I didn't know you would be here,' she observed, quite put out.

Mr van Tacx rose to his considerable height. 'Your mother was kind enough to offer me coffee,' he explained with what she realised was deceptive meekness. He pulled out a chair and she found herself sitting at the table, and a fine sight I must look, she thought crossly, my hair anyhow and this awful dressing gown. . . A garment kept at home for her visits; a cosy, rather shabby thing, useful for it's warmth and for donning for making the early morning tea and feeding the cat and letting Cuthbert out in the mornings, but hardly an enhancement to her person. She accepted a mug of coffee and sat glowering into it, unaware of Mr van Tacx's eyes upon her; there was a fine gleam in them, amused and something else.

He got up to go presently with a cordial good night to her parents and a casual, 'How about another visit to Stourhead tomorrow afternoon?' to her. She was on the point of refusing when he added in a tone of voice which immediately drew her mother's sympathy, 'My last chance, I expect, before I go back to Holland.'

'Oh, we shall miss you,' said Mrs Dowling, 'you seem quite one of the family, Julius. . .'

'I could not wish for anything better,' said Mr van Tacx, 'how kind of you to say so. For some reason I am attracted to Stourhead.'

He waited so obviously for an answer that Josephine forgot her wet hair and hideous dressing gown. 'Yes, all right, we'd better wear wellies, though.'

He nodded. His casual air masking his satisfaction at getting his own way. 'I'll collect you at two o'clock tomorrow.' He laid a large hand on her shoulder. 'Good night, Josephine.'

The feel of his hand was pleasant, more than that, comforting. She went to bed presently, to sleep soundly.

They went to church in the morning, but not before Dr Dowling had phoned Odstock and been told that all the victims of the accident were progressing; the parents were in intensive care and seriously injured and so was the tanker driver, but they were expected to recover.

The morning seemed brighter after that and at church Josephine sang the hymns with the gusto of relief and thankfulness. She had taken some extra care with her appearance to make up for the sight she must have presented on the previous evening, and it was vexing when Mr van Tacx did no more than glance at her as they went out of church.

But he was punctual enough; indeed, he had time to talk for a few minutes to her father while she wrapped herself against the cold and got into her rubber boots. The rain had ceased overnight. It was coldly damp and still wet underfoot, but the car was warm and once in it she felt loath to get out when they reached Stourhead. But once started, she forgot that; the lake was like a cold mirror, the island in its centre crowded with ducks, the wind sighing above their heads through the tall pines. The Old Man's beard still glistening with frozen rain and the hips and haws seemed redder than they were. Underfoot it was wet and in places very muddy, but it didn't matter. They walked briskly, talking of all manner of things, and Josephine for one, was very content with her company.

They didn't stop much; the afternoon was already dim and once the sun had set it would be difficult to find their way. They rounded the lake, made their way through the grottos and went through the gates as twilight descended on the little cottages beyond it.

'Let's go into the church?' suggested Mr van Tacx and took her arm. It was still open, the last of the daylight lighting up the stone knight on his tomb just inside the door. They wandered down the aisle and went into the tiny chapel on one side. They then wandered back towards the door and stopped by mutual consent to look back at the dim gentleness of the interior.

'I should like to be married here,' said Mr van Tacx surprisingly. And when Josephine gave him an amazed questioning look, 'To you, of course, Josephine.'

He sounded quite sure about it.

CHAPTER SIX

JOSEPHINE stood in the church porch gaping at her companion and he returned her look with a kind of placid amusement which stung her into saying: 'Well—whatever next?! What a thing to say.' And then at his raised eyebrows, she blushed crimson. 'I beg your pardon—I didn't mean to be rude, only I'm well. . .it was unexpected, what you said. And I couldn't possibly. . .'

She paused at a loss for words and Mr van Tacx said smoothly, 'Ah, you are of course being romantic—you dream of falling in love and swanning down the aisle in white satin.'

She considered this for a moment. 'I wouldn't mind not wearing white satin but I do think that being in love matters.'

'It didn't matter for you and Malcolm?' His voice was cool and silky.

'Nor you and your. . .' she exclaimed hotly.

'Magda,' he supplied without rancour, 'which rather strengthens my argument, doesn't it?'

He took her arm and began to walk down the path between the old grave stones. 'Compatibility and liking make a good marriage. One can fall out of love but liking is something which isn't easily changed. One could progress from liking to affection—a deep regard which would last a lifetime.'

Josephine stopped. 'You've thought about it,'

she said wonderingly, 'I mean you're not just talking idly.'

He smiled down at her and she found herself smiling back. 'Oh yes, I've thought about it, Josephine, and I want you to think about it too. And don't for God's sake make your mind up in a hurry. You can have all the time you want.

They were walking back towards the Spread Eagle car park. 'You really mean it?' said Josephine soberly.

His voice was harsh. 'My dear girl, I always mean what I say and I can promise you that I'll never say what I don't mean.'

She thought wistfully that he was telling her that he hadn't said a word about loving her. Well, at least he was being honest. And she liked him; he annoyed her, he was arrogant and he liked his own way, but he was kind and thoughtful of his patients and stood up without fuss to a crisis. He was good company too. He broke into her thoughts. 'No, Josephine, stop weighing pros and cons. Wait until I've gone.'

'Oh, you're going back to Holland?' She was conscious of disappointment. 'Not for good?'

He opened the car door and she got in. 'No,— I'll be back.' He got in beside her and started the engine.

He talked nothings as they drove back and the talk was general over tea, and if Josephine was rather silent no one remarked upon it. Only when he got up to go and her mother asked when they would see him again, he said quietly, 'I am going back to Holland, Mrs Dowling, but I hope that I shall see you shortly.' He bent and kissed her cheek and shook Dr Dowling's hand and looked across at Josephine standing on the other side of the hall. He was smiling faintly but he stayed where he was. He said softly *'Tots ziens*, Josephine,' and went out to his car.

Her father had gone out to the car with Mr van Tacx and her mother was containing her curiosity with the greatest difficulty. Josephine said carefully, 'I wonder what that means?' It irked her very much not to know and how like him to annoy her; he could at least have shaken her hand. I shall turn him down, she thought peevishly, it's all nonsense anyway. Her father came back indoors and she flounced into the kitchen and began to wash the tea things. Her day had gone sour. She pleaded a headache presently and went early to bed and in the morning she went back to St Michael's.

There was, naturally, no sign of Mr van Tacx, he had gone and although he had said that he would be back, her black mood denied that. It was during Mr Bull's round two days later, that he paused between patients to make some remark about Mr van Tacx. 'Splendid fellow,' he mumbled to no one in particular, 'glad he'll be back—very sound surgeon, brilliant in fact.'

'He's coming back?' asked Josephine in what she hoped was a casual manner.

'Lord, yes. It was only *tot ziens*.'

'What does that mean?' She felt a little wave of excitement at the prospect of knowing.

'Good Lord, girl, where are your wits. It means

so long—be seeing you—that kind of thing.'

'Oh,—oh, does it? I thought it might mean goodbye.'

Mr Bull snorted. 'Wondered what had got into you—face like a wet weekend. He'll be back by the end of the week.'

He took no notice of her confused mumbling but bent his attention upon the next patient.

It would make no difference even if he came back to England at the weekend, she would be on duty. She worked through the rest of the week and no one would have guessed from her calm pleasant manner how unsettled she felt. Saturday came and she imagined Mr van Tacx driving himself down to the Forsyths for the weekend. *'Tot ziens'* might mean so long, but it covered no specific time; a week, a month, even a year, and in a year's time, she mused, quite forgetting to be sensible, who knew what she would be doing or where she might be? A tricky question settled for her at the end of a long Sunday on duty. Joan was having her weekend off and she had had to send one of the more Senior Student nurses off with a sore throat which left her with a Third Year nurse who spent too little time getting on with the treatments and dressings and too much of it finding fault with the two very Junior nurses on duty with her. They were anxious to please and doing their best; Josephine sent her to her supper, bolstered up the nurses' flagging spirits, left them to tidy the ward for the night, shake up pillows and fetch drinks, and retired to her office to finish writing the report. There was no one very ill on the ward, the report was mostly routine, all the same she penned it carefully, went back to the ward to check a couple of drips and make sure, without appearing to do so, that the nurses were managing, and then went back again to her desk to start on the next fortnight's off duty. She found it a tiresome task, everyone had to have two days off in each week and over and above that, she had to be sure that the nurses on duty were a good mixture of junior and senior, especially on operation days, and another thing, Mr Bull had strong likes and dislikes. She had to take care that those he took exception to were off duty on round days. She had her head in her hands, trying to get the pattern just right when the door opened on the briefest of knocks and Mr van Tacx walked in.

His hullo was quiet but his glance was warmly friendly. Josephine felt an upsurge of pleasure at the sight of him although she kept her pen poised; the night staff would be on in ten minutes and she was by no means finished. He saw that and smiled a little. 'I want to talk to you. I'll wait at the entrance—don't bother to change—just put on your cloak.' He nodded briskly and went away, leaving her, as he so often did, with her mouth open and no chance to speak.

'I shan't go,' she muttered and went back to the off duty, which quite suddenly resolved itself into exactly what she had wanted. That gave her time to make her final round before the night nurses arrived and for once there were no hold-ups; the patients were quiet and nicely settled, the nurses were on duty punctually and the report was given without interruption. She had already sent the day staff off duty and there was no reason why she should stay. She picked up the roomy bag she took on duty with her each day, slung her cloak round her shoulders and went off duty herself.

She had said that she wouldn't go with Julius van Tacx but somehow her treacherous feet bore her down to the entrance hall, to find him leaning against a wall, his hands in his pockets, quite obviously waiting for her.

'I've not even combed my hair,' she told him fiercely.

'I like you just as well with uncombed hair,' he told her placidly and propelled her through the door and into the Bentley.

'Where are we going, and why?' Demanded Josephine.

'I have a small flat and I did tell you—we have to talk.'

'What about?' she persisted.

'Us. Now sit back and relax for a few minutes. Have you had your supper?'

'No.'

He was driving through the quiet Sunday streets, going west through the city. 'I thought you lived in Holland. . .'

'I do—that is my home, but I've bought a pied-a-terre here; I come over quite often and it's convenient.'

He had no more to say and she occupied herself in watching where they were going. Through Bloomsbury and still going west then crossing the Tottenham Court Road and turning into New

Cavendish Street and then into Wimpole Street. He stopped the car half way down a terrace of narrow Georgian houses and got out to open her door. She looked around her as he locked the car; the door before her was a handsome one with a row of brass plates on the wall beside it. There was a light from the street lamp which was enough to see Mr van Taxc's name on the bottom one, and she said in surprise, 'Oh, you've got rooms here. . .'

He unlocked the door and urged her gently inside. 'Yes, but my flat's on the top floor. There's a lift.'

'I thought you had a service flat.'

'I bought this one from a friend; we shall need a home from home, shan't we?' A remark which left her speechless.

The lift door opened on to a small landing with a door facing them, Mr van Taxc unlocked the door and stood aside to let her go past him. The hall was small, panelled in some dark wood and thickly carpeted. There were doors on either side and passages to left and right. He opened one of the doors and ushered her into a long low room overlooking the street. It was panelled to shoulder height and furnished with a vast sofa, easy chairs and several small tables, with some nice silver and china scattered around. A charming room, and Josephine said so in a rather high artificial voice, anxious not to appear ill at ease.

'You like it? Good. I enjoyed furnishing the place but of course you must alter anything you don't fancy.'

She turned to look at him. 'Look, Julius—aren't you taking everything for granted? You—you went off back to Holland without a word, and now here you. . .'

'Well, of course I'm here. Did I not say that I would be back. And did I not say that you should have a few days in which to make up your mind? And have you?'

She hesitated. 'I don't know anything about you. Where do you live? And have you a family? And are you sure that you really want to marry me? I mean you could so easily fall in love. . .'

He took her cloak and pulled a chair forward and pushed her gently into it. 'I live near Leiden; quite a small village but near enough to go into Leiden and the Hague and Amsterdam, to be able to get to hospital easily. A pleasant house I have always thought, but then I was brought up there— it's old and there's a garden. My mother died last year and my father lives in Leiden—a retired surgeon, although he still lectures from time to time. I have three sisters all married and two brothers, the elder is at Edinburgh Royal Infirmary—a Junior House Surgeon, and the younger is still in medical school in Leiden. And yes, Josephine, I am quite sure that I want to marry you.'

She asked why and waited with inward excitement for his answer.

He said easily. 'Did I not make that clear? We have both failed in our attempts to marry for love; we have much to offer each other—you said that you didn't like me but I believe that you like me well enough now; we have so much in common, we enjoy each other's company, don't we? We can spend time in each other's company without wishing ourselves elsewhere. You understand my work, you won't throw tantrums when I come home late, you may even listen patiently while I discuss it with you. We are once bitten twice shy, are we not, and not anxious to be hurt again. So we shall marry and get to know each other slowly and when we feel that we can live together as man and wife we'll do so, but only then. It sounds a little cold perhaps but it need not be, we shall be warmed by friendship and what I hope will be affection. In time of course.'

He got up. 'I'll get some coffee and sandwiches while you sit and think about it.'

She said instantly, 'Oh, let me. . .'

'I make good coffee, besides I have a daily housekeeper who will have left everything ready.'

He went away and she could hear him whistling from somewhere down the hall. Presently he came back with a laden tray; coffee in a silver pot, fine china and a silver platter piled with sandwiches.

'Be mother?' He invited, and when they had had their coffee and he had passed her the sandwiches, 'I have to give a series of lectures at Leeds Royal Infirmary in three weeks time. I thought we might marry first; you can drive up with me. We'll stay in York and I can go to and fro—I shall be there a week and you'll be on your own for most of the day, but York is interesting and so beautiful and there are some good shops, I daresay you could fill in your days.

'I have to give in my resignation,' began Josephine weakly.

'Oh, I'll take care of that. If I arrange for you to leave in a week's time will that be sufficient for you to get fixed up for the wedding?'

She blinked up at him. 'My goodness you do rush along, don't you? I haven't said I'll marry you. . .'

He said deliberately: 'Will you marry me, Josephine?'

She heard herself saying 'Yes, though I daresay I'll wake up in the middle of the night and wonder if I'm mad,' she added, 'I mean it's all a bit crazy.'

'Not nearly as crazy as if you had married Malcolm knowing that you didn't love him, or I had married Magda.'

She acknowledged that gravely. 'The French still arrange their marriages, I believe—I knew a girl—she was at school with me, and she went back to France and married the man her parents had picked out for her. I went to visit her; she was very happy and content.'

She gave him a steady look from her beautiful eyes. 'I shall do my best to be a good wife, Julius.'

He leaned across and took her hand in his. 'Yes, I know that. I don't know if I shall be a good husband but I will care for you and make sure that your life is a happy one.'

'Why won't you be a good husband?'

'I'm intolerant and sometimes bad tempered, I don't suffer fools gladly and I'm impatient.'

She smiled: 'You forget that I've had several years of Mr Bull and now you. . .'

He laughed then and she laughed with him. 'I'll see your office people in the morning—when will you be going home again?'

'This weekend.'

'I'll drive you down. I said that I would like to get married in Stourton Church, will you agree to that?'

'Yes, of course. Do we want a very quiet wedding?'

'That's for you to say, Josephine,' he smiled. 'I should like my father there and brothers and sisters, they'll bring their husbands of course, and the Forsyths too.'

'And Joan and Matt, and Joan and Natalie for bridesmaids and Mr Bull. . .'

She drew a deep breath. 'I should really like to wear white satin. Would you mind very much?' I promise you we won't invite too many guests.'

'I should like you to wear white satin too, my dear.' His voice was kind and understanding. Can you fix everything up in three weeks?'

'I think so. Don't we have to put up the banns or something?'

'I'll get a special licence.' He sounded friendly and so casual and most comfortably matter-of-fact. 'If you leave in a week—your weekend anyway, isn't it? You'll have just a fortnight. . . Time enough?'

'If I 'phone Mother. . .'

'You can do that now, that would give her a week to start the preliminaries.

He made it all seem so easy and simple. And her mother and Father hadn't seemed in the least surprised. Julius took her back to St Michael's presently, wished her good night at the entrance, kissed her briefly on a cheek and waited until she had gone through the door to the nurses home. She undressed and showered and got into bed, determined to lie quietly and go over everything they had said that evening. Perhaps she was making the greatest mistake of her life. She didn't stay awake long enough to find out. And in the morning she discovered that she had no doubts at all.

She said nothing to her friends over breakfast; supposing—just supposing Julius didn't go to the office? Supposing he had had second thoughts? She went on duty and buried herself in her work, determined not to think about it.

It was Matt who settled things for her. He was half way through his round during the morning when he said, 'Mr van Tacx told me the news this morning, Jo. I wish you all the best—you'll make a splendid couple. When's the wedding?'

She blushed. 'In three weeks, before Julius goes to Leeds. You'll come, won't you, Matt? I'm going to ask Joan to be a bridesmaid, you could drive her down.'

He beamed at her. 'Does she know?'

'Not yet. I'll tell her when we have a few minutes to ourselves.'

'You'll leave, of course?'

'Yes. I'll suggest that Joan takes over; she's ready for a ward.'

'Until she gets married.' They smiled at each other without speaking and finished the round.

She was summoned to the office shortly afterwards. The Principal Nursing Officer wasn't best pleased that an experienced Sister was to be wrested from her at a moment's notice, but Julius, Josephine reflected, must have twisted that lady's arm. She wondered what arguments he had employed, replied to her superior's measured observations, and took herself back to the ward. Her boats were burnt now and she might as well tell everyone. Joan listened round eyed and delighted. 'Oh, Sister, how marvellous, and me a bridesmaid too. What shall I wear?'

'I hadn't thought—my sister, Natalie, will be the other one. Something warm looking—it's November and it's bound to rain. Velvet I think, a nice claret colour, perhaps. We'll have to look for something ready made, there's no time. . .'

'And you, you'll wear white?' breathed Joan.

'Me, oh yes. At least cream—white's a bit stark isn't it? I'll 'phone Natalie this evening and see what she thinks—if she doesn't mind, we'll wangle an afternoon off together and try and find something to suit you both. There's only a week. . .'

They stared at each other, thinking of all the dozens of things which would have to be done in those few days. Josephine, off duty that evening, spent it making neat lists while her friends gave advice, discussed her future and reiterated her great good fortune. Rather to her surprise, she found herself agreeing with them; she was being swept off her feet and it felt rather nice; instead of waiting soberly while plans were made, discussed and as like as not discarded, she was being married out of hand within weeks. If they had been in love it would have been romantic, she thought wistfully.

But there was nothing romantic about her meeting with Julius the next morning. He arrived for the round looking as aloof as always, his good-morning to her was uttered in a polite, cool voice and the look he gave her was brief and detached. She was a girl of spirit. She replied in a voice which wasn't just cool but iced round the edges, failing to see the laughter in his eyes. Her correctness throughout the round was exemplary and if Joan had hoped for some small glimpse of romance she was doomed to disappointment. The round over, they repaired to the office, coffee as usual, Josephine thought and found herself wrong. 'Matt,' said Mr van Tacx easily, 'take Joan to the linen cupboard or something and have your coffee will you?' I want to talk to Josephine.'

He took the tray from Mrs Cross and closed the door gently. 'Now we can be ourselves,' he observed placidly. 'I must say I find it difficult to call you Sister Dowling. It has never come easily to my tongue, now it's almost impossible.' He smiled with a charm to light his whole face. 'And you, my dear with a poker up your back—are you going to call me sir after we are married?'

Josephine sat down and poured their coffee, suddenly light hearted. 'Of course not, I was being professional.'

He bent and kissed her gently. 'You terrified me. Has the Office contacted you?'

'Yes, I'm to leave on Saturday after lunch, so that Joan can have her days off first and be back to take over for the weekend.'

'Good. I've applied for the licence and told my family.' He put down his coffee cup and put a hand into a pocket. 'And there's this. . .'

He gave her a small leather box and when she opened it there was a ring inside. Rose diamonds, exquisitely set in an intricate gold mounting. 'My mother's. I fetched it when I went home the other week. She wanted me to have it and for my bride to wear it.'

She took the ring from the box and held it out to him. 'It's a very beautiful ring and I'll always wear it. Will you put it on, Julius?'

It fitted and she turned her pretty capable hand to and fro, admiring the stones' gleam. 'Thank you, Julius, I. . .' The 'phone interrupted her and she lifted the receiver. 'For you,' she said, and handed it over.

The conversation was brief. 'I'll be in the accident room if I'm wanted,' he told her. 'There's a criminal abortion just brought in.'

He had gone, his coffee half drunk, leaving her to sit and look at her lovely ring. Presently she put it back in the box and put the box in her pocket, took the tray back to the kitchen and went into the ward to check the dressings the third year nurse was doing. She did this very competently and with her usual composure. Neither the two nurses doing the dressing or the lady in the bed had the faintest inkling that the ring, safely out of sight, was nevertheless sending waves of excitement through her calm person.

Her full day drew to a close, she hadn't seen Julius again, but then hadn't expected to. She and Joan put their heads together, decided on an afternoon when they could go shopping together, and after she had given the report, she went off duty. She would spend her evening, she had decided happily, 'phoning her mother and Natalie, and deciding what clothes she would need to buy.

As it turned out, she spent her evening quite differently. Julius was waiting for her as she crossed the entrance hall. 'Mrs Twigg's left supper ready,' he told her without preamble. 'We'll get the details settled, shall we? And you can 'phone your mother for as long as you like.'

'Ten minutes while I change,' said Josephine, breathlessly, and sped away to her room, where she showered and dragged on a tweed suit, surrounded for most of the time by several of her friends. She was a little more than ten minutes for the ring had to be admired.

Mrs Twigg was a splendid cook, and judging from the beautifully polished silver and shining glass on the circular table in the dining room of the flat, she was a treasure of the first water. Josephine, nicely mellowed by a glass of Sercial, ate Vichyssoise, *poulet chausseur*, and chocolate orange creams with an appetite induced by a day's hard work and helped along by the bottle of champagne Julius produced. And while they ate they discussed their plans for the wedding with an almost impersonal efficiency. Hours later, in bed,

Josephine wondered if there was another couple in the land who had arranged a marriage in such a businesslike fashion. Yet she had found it much more to her liking than the plans she had made with Malcolm. At least he had made the plans and she had most uncharacteristically agreed, whereas Julius had listened courteously to her own ideas and had never once tried to have his own way. Surely a good augury for a harmonious future? She had talked to her mother at great length too and that lady made it very apparent that she had no doubts about that future. Moreover, she had telephoned her sister and naturally that had been lengthy too. The question of the bridesmaid's dresses was a serious one not to be dealt with too hastily. Julius had sat back in one of his comfortable chairs, smoking a pipe and showing no signs of impatience. In all, a very satisfactory evening. Josephine turned over in bed and went to sleep. She woke once in the night to reflect that Julius had kissed her quite warmly, but rather like an old friend, she might have worried about that if she hadn't fallen asleep again.

The week went swiftly; he had told her that he wouldn't see her until he came to drive her to her home sometime during Saturday afternoon. She hadn't asked why, she supposed that he had gone back to Holland and there was plenty to stop her wondering about it. She and Joan had spent a hectic afternoon shopping for bridesmaid's dresses and found what they had in mind at Laura Ashley's; cotton velvet in a deep claret, just right for grey November days. Luckily Natalie was a size ten like Joan; Josephine bought the dresses and then, feeling reckless, purchased several pretty voile blouses for herself as well as a dark blue viyella check with a demure white collar and cuffs. It was a good start, she considered, but she would have to come up to London again and find a dress for herself.

She dismissed her own affairs from her mind and went back to an evening's hard work, and once she was off duty, her packing.

The ward was tolerably quiet, she went round saying goodbye to her patients on Saturday morning, paid a visit to the office, where she was offered guarded good wishes and then during her dinner hour, bade goodbye to her friends. She was ready by two o'clock, her luggage in the hall, and a pile of presents heaped beside it. She had been rather overwhelmed by the gifts she had received; she and Julius could open them together when they got home. Quite a few of her friends had arranged to come to her wedding and since Julius was driving her down, she had left her Mini for Mercy to bring down on the wedding day, several of them had cars and transport was no problem. She took a careful look at herself in the looking glass, glanced round her room for the last time and went along to the Sisters' sitting room. Julius hadn't said at what time he would pick her up and she had forgotten to ask.

She didn't have to wait for long. There was a 'phone call from the lodge within five minutes of her settling in a chair, asking her to go to the front entrance. Feeling suddenly shy and uncertain, she went through the familiar passages, rather absurdly worrying about Joan and the ward and the patients, and just as she reached the door to the entrance hall, beset by doubts as to whether she was making a frightful mistake, giving up a life she knew like the back of her hand, a successful career and a loving home to go to, and for what? An almost unknown future with a man who, however much he liked her, didn't love her. Then she opened the door and saw Julius leaning against the lodge, talking to the porter, and without quite understanding why she forgot her doubts.

For a man about to be married, Julius was remarkably calm. He greeted her with the casualness of an old friend and since her luggage was already stowed in the boot, all she had to do was to say goodbye to the porter and get into the car. Their departure was enlivened by the appearance of several of her friends' heads at the nearest windows and cries of good luck and see you at the wedding, and she waved back; rather to her surprise, Julius waved too.

'Are you staying with the Forsyths?' she asked.

'Just for the night. I must get back to Leiden; I've a list on Monday morning.'

'You didn't come over just to drive me down?'

'Yes, I did.' He gave her a wide smiling glance. 'Your mother has crumpets for tea; she's determined to anglicise me. I'm to stay for supper too.'

'Oh, good.' Her shyness had gone, she was completely at ease with him. 'Will you be back before the wedding?'

'Next weekend if I can manage it. Just for a

night. I'll bring my father over when I come the day before we are to be married—the rest of the family will come on their own. I've taken over the rooms at the Spread Eagle. Your mother offered to have some of them, but I'm sure you have aunts and uncles and so forth. I think your mother is rather enjoying herself.'

'I'm sure she is. It's nice doing it all in a rush, though. There's a lack of time. . .' She stopped and bit her lip.

'To have second thoughts,' he finished for her placidly. 'No there isn't. Have you had second thoughts, Josephine?'

'Well, no, actually, I haven't.' She added in faint alarm: 'You haven't have you?'

He laughed. 'No, certainly not. Are you going to miss St Michael's?'

She shook her head. 'It's a funny thing, but I don't believe I shall give it another thought.'

They settled down to a gentle chat about the church and what kind of flowers she wanted and what his family intended to do while they were staying at Stourton. The journey went quickly; Josephine could have sat happily enough for another few hours, talking about nothing much, but in what seemed to her no time at all they were stopping at her home and her father was at the door to welcome them.

Natalie and Mike were home for the weekend and there was a small flurry of greetings and kisses with Cuthburt pushing among them and even Mrs Whisker winding herself around their legs. They had a lovely buttery tea together round the fire, with many cups of tea and Mrs Dowling's fairy cakes to follow the crumpets, and later after supper Julius got up to go. He shook the doctor's hand, clapped Mike on the shoulder, kissed his hostess and Natalie and then, a smile twitching the corner of his mouth, followed a rather self-conscious Josephine into the hall. Here he took her deliberately in his arms and kissed her soundly. 'I'm only doing what is expected of me,' he told her blandly as he let her go.

She stayed there until the sound of the car had faded into the distance: she had enjoyed the kiss but she wasn't quite happy about his remark. Had he really only kissed her because everyone expected him to do so, or had he enjoyed it too? After all, she reasoned, they could be fond of each other without being in love, and people who liked each other kissed, didn't they?

She went back to the sitting room and was at once drawn into talk about the wedding.

Beyond agreeing to her mother's plans for the reception, arguing the merits of a velvet toque rather than a felt hat for her mother's wedding headpiece, assuring her father that his elderly morning coat still fitted him splendidly, she spent the first three days at home in a soporific haze, helping around the house, tramping miles with a delighted Cuthbert, sitting by the fire, doing nothing. But on the fourth day she bestirred herself, cozened Mrs Bagg to see to her father's lunch, wheedled him into driving her and her mother to Tisbury early in the morning, and went up to town. In the train they made more lists, took an extravagent taxi to Regent Street and got down to a day's shopping. Mrs Dowling's hat was the first thing on the list; a vital piece of headgear which had to be exactly what she wanted. They were lucky enough to find it within half an hour and after that everything was plain sailing. A smart wool two-piece was found to go with the hat; gloves handbag and shoes, all obtained in the same shop, completed the outfit and the ladies restored their strength with coffee and cakes before making for Bond Street and then Sloane Square.

Josephine, with a nest egg in the bank and a generous cheque from her father, could afford to be choosey. They prowled from shop to shop until she found what she wanted. Satin, thick and lustrous and the colour of rich cream, very simply made, with long tight sleeves and a high round neck. It fitted her, and that was a miracle for she was a splendidly built girl and she had found that fashion frowned on anyone of her shape and size. But there it was, a perfect fit and a matching veil and a little coronet of orange blossom to go with it. She paid its high price without turning a hair and went in search of white satin slippers.

They were laden by now and stopped for lunch, and since they had found their way to Harrods it seemed a good idea to look for something suitable to go away in. She found it almost at once, a rich brown tweed suit and a silk blouse to go with it, and while she was about it, a dashing felt hat. They called it a day then, had a cup of tea and caught a train back to Tisbury, and since it was dark and the doctor would be busy in the surgery, they took a taxi home.

A most successful day, they agreed, as they got the supper. 'I'll get shoes in Salisbury,' said Josephine, 'and see if Country Casuals have a dress or two,' and she looked surprised when her mother laughed softly.

'I was just thinking,' said Mrs Dowling, 'of Malcolm's mother. She wouldn't have approved.' She added unexpectedly: 'You don't think of him any more, love? I know you are marrying Julius. . .'

Josephine was used to her Mother's disconcerting remarks. 'Haven't thought about him for weeks,' she said truthfully and eyed her mother steadily. 'I'm marrying Julius and I'm content, Mother.'

He arrived on Saturday, just as he said he would, and stayed the night. He brought flowers for Mrs Dowling, spent an hour or more with Dr Dowling in his study and took Josephine for a long walk in the icy cold afternoon, Cuthbert prancing clumsily in front of them. They were to go to Stourton after tea, he told her, and have a chat with the vicar.

'Just to see that everything's as it should be. Did the rector here mind that you weren't marrying from your own church?'

'No, not a bit. He is going to assist.'

'Splendid we'll see him in the morning after church.'

'You won't have to go back tomorrow—you can stay a day or two?'

The faintest of smiles lighted his face when he

heard the unconscious eagerness in her voice.

'I'll have to go back in the evening—I'll catch a night ferry.'

'And you'll come here next weekend?' They had stopped to look at the wintry landscape over a five barred gate.

'Impossible, I'm afraid. It'll be the day before the wedding. I'll give you a ring, though.'

She had to be content with that, and with the message from his family and a charming letter, written in a beautifully clear, spidery hand from his father. They went to Stourton in the evening and spent an hour with the vicar and paid a brief visit to the church. They stood together by the knight's grave and she was glad when Julius took her hand in his and held it close; a kind of promise that everything was going to be all right.

Everyone looked at them in church in the morning, nodding and smiling and whispering to each other. A good many of those there would get in their cars and go over to Stourton for the wedding; it was a pity, they told each other that Josephine wasn't to marry in her own village, but they made allowances for the bridegroom's wishes; he was, after all, a foreigner. And so very good looking. . .

The rest of the day went too quickly, in no time at all she was standing in the hall once more, bidding him goodbye. Her mother had insisted that he should bring his family to dinner on the evening before the wedding and he said now, 'It won't be too much? There will be nine of us. . .'

'Mother will love it; she's a marvellous hostess;

she sort of wafts her way through it all and nothing ever goes wrong.'

'And you, Josephine, will you waft your way through the wedding?'

She took him seriously. 'I'm not like Mother, but I won't let you down.' She added earnestly. 'I think we shall be happy together. I mean compatibility and all that.'

He agreed with her with a grave face and a decided twinkle in his eyes. And his kiss was entirely satisfactory.

CHAPTER SEVEN

JOSEPHINE stood in front of the cheval glass in her mother's bedroom and studied her person. Her reflection stared back at her; a serene image in cream satin, the orange blossom coronet perched on top of her high piled chestnut locks. Not bad, she decided, not bad at all; at least she wouldn't let Julius down before his family. For some reason, his family had assumed the proportions of an ogre-like hierachy, ready to pounce on her if she didn't conform to their standards. It was a pity, she reflected, that she hadn't given a little more thought to them. Marrying Julius was one thing; she liked him, but would his family like her?

She turned away from the glass and sat down on her mother's bed. She supposed that all brides had a last moment of doubt and she was having it now. She put up her hand to make a minute adjustment to the coronet; at least there would be no mother-in-law to cast a disparaging eye over her clothes. And father-in-law. . .her thoughts were brought to an end by the entry of her brides-maids, flushed and excited. The pair of them looked delightful and she was glad that she had chosen the warm glowing claret velvet; it cheered up the grey day outside. They had arranged their hair in an identical style and tied it with matching ribbons and the effect was charming. They chorused their admiration of Josephine's appearance, kissed her carefully so that they didn't disarrange anything, and flew downstairs to the waiting car, their place taken almost at once by her mother, looking exactly as the bride's mother should look and searching fruitlessly for her glasses.

'Round your neck on a chain, Mother,' advised Josephine patiently. 'You do look smashing.'

'So do you, darling. Being a bride suits you—Julius is such a lucky man—I told him so, and he agreed. Of course, one would expect him to.'

She too kissed the bride and went unhurriedly downstairs to where the chauffeur was waiting behind the wheel. Being a local man he knew Mrs Dowling well and had allowed for her being unpunctual. She was settled in with the bridesmaids and off they went. Mike had already gone with Matt and now there were only Josephine and her father and Mrs Bagg, wearing a surprising hat and a new overall for the occasion, bustling around chivvying the hired waiters who were to serve at the reception.

She went downstairs presently and got into the car with her father. 'Nervous?' he wanted to know.

'Well, yes. . .'

He chuckled. 'I'm willing to bet my fees for a month that Julius is feeling even worse.'

Josephine hadn't thought of that; the idea of Julius feeling anything other than coolly capable of dealing with any situation which might arise, hadn't entered her head. She felt a lot better and by the time they reached the church she felt quite herself again, just as capable as he was to deal with the future.

The little church was packed and despite the gloomy morning, a quite sizable crowd had gathered outside its doors. Josephine tucked an arm into her father's and walked up the stone path to the church door where Natalie and Mary were waiting. The organ was playing very loudly and the church was full but there wasn't time to look around her. Julius had his back to her, looking larger than ever in his morning coat. She supposed that the younger man beside him was one of his brothers. She took a deep calming breath and nipped her father's arm and they started their walk down the aisle. Julius turned round then and smiled at her, it was wholly friendly and comforting and the small pinpricks of doubt she had been fighting all the morning disappeared. He took her hand as she reached his side and gave it a reassuring squeeze as the service began.

Everything would be all right.

The next few hours were a pleasant blur; they had driven back to her home, sitting side by side in the back of the wedding car and Julius had taken her hand in his and talked about the wedding in a perfectly normal matter-of-fact manner. They had barely time to station themselves in her mother's drawing room before the first of the family and guests arrived. And as she knew from the previous evening Julius's father wasn't in the least alarming; he was an elderly edition of his son and just as tall and large. He had kissed her heartily and said all the right things in a warm

manner before allowing his two sons to take his
place. Gelmar and Eduard, younger, slightly
smaller editions of Julius. They hugged and kissed
her in a brotherly fashion, delighted that she was
exactly the sister-in-law they had always wanted
and then made room for his sisters: Lelia, tall and
blonde and pretty with a solid pleasant faced man
at her shoulder—Huib, then Alodia, very like her
sister but younger and not quite as fair. Her husband was tall and thin and with a grave face—
Jon. And lastly Isa, baby of the family, still in her
early twenties and married to a cheerful round
faced young man whom she addressed as Robert.
'There are so many of us,' she told Josephine,
'and Lelia and Alodia have children and there are
aunts and uncles. I think we shall all like you
very much—you're so pretty and we will have
fun together when we meet.' She stood on tip toe
to kiss Julius. 'Now you are married you will not
work so hard,' she told him coaxingly, 'and we
will all come for weekends and you will come and
visit us.' She smiled engagingly at Josephine. 'He
has been a bachelor for too long; we have begged
him to marry and always he says perhaps, perhaps,
and now he has and I for one am very pleased.'

They had cut the cake and drunk champagne
and had their photographs taken and presently she
had gone up to her room with Natalie and Joan
and changed into her new suit, and still not quite
believing it all, she had got into the car beside
Julius and been driven away, with half the village
there to wave them goodbye. Not that they would
be gone for all that length of time; in just over a

week they would be back again to collect the rest of her luggage and travel on to Holland. She wished that she could have had more time with Julius's family. She had liked them and she thought that they had liked her, but presumably there would be time enough to get to know them better. She remembered vaguely that her mother had said something about paying old Mr van Tacx a visit later on and Natalie and Mike had both been invited to stay with Lelia.

She broke the silence as Julius drove steadily towards the A303. 'Where does Lelia live?'

'Den Hague—Alodia lives in Friesland and Isa in Groningen. Gelmar and Eduard still live with my father in Leiden.' He glanced at her and smiled. 'Did you, find them rather overpowering?'

'No—they're nice. I like your father too. He's like you, only older.'

He said softly, 'Thank you, Josephine,' and she blushed a little.

After a moment she said. 'It was a good wedding, wasn't it?'

'Splendid. Something to remember for the rest of our lives. You're not tired?'

She shook her head. 'My goodness no. But it was all rather—rather unusual, I'm not quite sure it's all happened.'

'If you mean you aren't sure if we're married, we are. You made a charming and quite beautiful bride, Josephine.'

'Thank you. You weren't so bad yourself. And I haven't thanked you for your wedding present. It's quite lovely.' She touched the pearls at her neck with a gentle finger. 'I've never had such a lovely gift.'

'I'm glad you like it and that you wore it at our wedding. My mother wore it too, and her mother before her.'

They had joined the A303 and were racing along steadily. 'I'm making for St Albans and the A1. We'll stop for tea once we're on it and get to York in time for a latish dinner. I have to lecture tomorrow afternoon which gives us the morning to take a look round and for you to get your bearings.'

She had hoped that he would ask her to go with him to Leeds, but it seemed that he had no such idea. And it was the last thing she would suggest. She agreed in her pleasant voice and remarked on the comfort of the car.

'It gets me around,' he agreed laconically. 'You'll have a car of your own, of course.'

She murmured thanks; presumably there weren't to be many occasions when they would be together. Well, she had known that, hadn't she? They would go slowly at first, getting to know each other, not infringing on the other's privacy. They had, after all, all their lives before them, and they were starting out on a sound basis, mutual regard and liking, and what had he said? Compatability, surely better than a sudden falling in love which could so easily die without these three things?

The time passed pleasantly; they talked a little and their silences were just as pleasant. They gained St Albans and took to the A1 and presently stopped for tea, and after that they kept up a steady speed which got them to York in the early evening.

Josephine hadn't thought much of the country on the way up, although she was willing to concede that a main road, running through industrial areas, was hardly conducive to splendid scenery, but she was enchanted with the city when they reached it. The tree-lined road leading to the city walls was splendid and her first sight of Micklegate drew a pleased sound from her.

'Unexpected, isn't it?' asked Julius. 'Our hotel is just across the street from the Minister. I think you'll like it.'

Once through the Micklegate the streets were narrow and busy but when they reached the hotel it was to find a surprising quiet. It was dark by now, and cold, and Josephine was glad to go inside the hotel and be taken up to her room. They were on the first floor with a bathroom between them, overlooking the open space between the hotel and the Minster.

'Don't bother to change,' Julius advised her, wandering in from his room. 'I'll come for you in ten minutes, shall I? We'll have dinner and if you aren't too tired I'll give you an idea of the times I'll be working while we are here.'

A strange kind of day, thought Josephine sleepily as she curled up in bed later, but one that she had enjoyed. A girl's wedding day was supposed to be the most marvellous one of her life and thinking about it, she had to agree. Which in it's way was strange for neither she nor Julius were in love, although there was no denying the fact that she enjoyed his company and as far as she knew he liked hers. They had had a delightful dinner together and then, warmly clad against the cold night, she had gone with him, her hand tucked in his arm, walking the quiet streets round the Minster, not talking much. He had wished her good night when they got back to the hotel and kissed her lightly and she had gone upstairs to bed happily enough. They were behaving like two sensible people and she for one was content to let it be so.

They went out directly after breakfast the next morning into a cold and gloomy day which neither of them minded about. Since the Minster was, so to speak, on their doorstep they went there first, the nine hundred year old building, even though part of it was being repaired after the fire, was, in Josephine's opinion, worth several hours of prowling, but now they wandered round with an eye on the clock since Julius would be going to Leeds after an early lunch, and there was so much else to see.

They had coffee in an upmarket café in one of the narrow streets lined with the kind of shops to tempt any woman, but she wasn't allowed to waste time on them, 'You can look your fill when you are on your own,' Julius pointed out firmly, and stopped suddenly to put a hand in his pocket. 'You'll need some money,' he observed matter-of-factly.

'I've got some,' Josephine began awkwardly to be cut short by his curt: 'I daresay you have, but you are my wife now; you'll have an allowance once we get to Holland, in the meantime spend what you want to.'

He took her purse from her and stuffed some notes inside. He didn't seem to notice her embarrassment but took her arm with the remark that they might see something to take back for her mother. They paused to look in an antique jewellers and he pointed out a blue enamel and pearl brooch. 'Something like that,' he suggested.

Josephine examined the price tag. 'It's three hundred pounds,' she pointed out with patient amusement.

He gave her a quick look. 'We haven't got around to a talk about money, have we?' He wanted to know quietly. 'I have more than enough, my dear.'

She stared up at him. 'You mean to buy a brooch like that—like I'd buy a box of chocolates?'

He nodded. 'But you'd rather not buy it? We'll find something else. We'll go down here and walk through the Shambles, it's full of enchanting little shops.'

They strolled along, not minding about the weather, peering into the shop windows, and presently went back to the hotel and had lunch.

'What shall you do this afternoon?' Julius wanted to know.

'Oh, go out again, I think. I must find something for Natalie and Wendy and there are Mike and Father and Mother. You have to lecture tomorrow morning, don't you?'

'Yes, and I'm afraid I have to stay to lunch. We'll go out and have tea when I get back; perhaps

there'll be time to go to the museum at the Castle.'
He glanced at his watch. 'I must be off, I should
be back by six o'clock.'

He left her sitting over her coffee, feeling
strangely forlorn.

She shook the feeling off, had another cup of
coffee and went to her room for her coat and
gloves. There was plenty to see in York, she
reminded herself vigorously, an afternoon shopping would be pleasant. Before she left the room
she looked in her purse. The notes were still
crumpled up inside it and she smoothed them out
and counted them. She counted them again just to
make sure; Julius must have made a mistake, she
held enough money in her hand to buy the blue
enamel brooch twice over. She tucked all but a
hundred pounds into an inner pocket and set out
feeling rich.

The afternoon was already darkening, but the
shops were glowing with Christmas goods. She
spent an ecstatic hour in Culpepper's shop, sniff-
ing at soaps and lotions and choosing carefully,
before finding a bookshop where she discovered
a newly published suspense novel by her father's
favourite author. Liberty's might be a happy hunt-
ing ground, and she remembered passing the shop
during the morning and on the way she went into
Crabtree and Evelyn's and bought more lotions
and soaps. Liberty's overflowed with the kind of
things she had so often admired but never bought
because they were extravagent trifles, and
although she longed to have them they weren't
actually useful. She let herself go now, telling

herself that the lacey beribboned boxes and little dolls, the beflowered photo frames and the delicate scarves were ideal presents for her friends at St Michaels. A bit shocked at the amount of money she had spent from the hundred pounds, she took herself off for tea in one of those faintly Edwardian tea rooms almost impossible to find nowadays, where she drank tea from thin china and ate a buttered muffin and, since she was still hungry, a mountainous cream cake. It was dark by now and after five o'clock. She walked back to the hotel and went up to her room; she would fill in an hour by having a bath and doing her nails. She laid her purchases on the bed, filled the bath to the brim, poured in the best of Culpepper's bath oil, and lay in the fragrant warmth, contemplating the evening ahead of her with pleasure.

She was in her dressing gown, brushing her hair, when there was a knock on the door and Julius came in.

Josephine put down her brush. 'You're early. How nice. Do you want tea? Was your lecture a success?'

He studied the bed carefully, made room for himself among all the parcels and sat down. 'I skipped tea but I don't want any, thanks. The lecture went off well enough.' He smiled lazily at her. 'You look nice.'

Her face flushed from her hot bath, became even more so. 'Oh—not really, I haven't done my face or my hair.'

She picked up the brush again and began brushing once more; it gave her something to do and she was feeling awkward again. 'I've had a lovely afternoon,' she ventured. Then remembering suddenly. 'Julius, you must have made a mistake when you put that money in my bag. I took a hundred pounds and I've spent an awful lot of it. I've got the rest of it though, it's tucked away in my purse. . .'

'I didn't make a mistake, Josephine, the money is for you to spend how you wish.' And at her small sound of protest; 'Don't say anymore about it. What did you buy?'

She told him, feeling vaguely resentful of his high-handedness, but if he noticed that he said nothing and presently he went away to his room with the casual remark that he would be back in half an hour.

By the time he returned she had convinced herself that she had been unnecessarily touchy. Matters would sort themselves out once they were in Holland and she knew about his way of life. Strangely enough she hadn't given much thought to that; that he had enough to live on was apparent but now it seemed as though he had more than that.

She dressed carefully, putting on one of the new dresses she had bought, a dark green crêpe with a tucked bodice and a wide pleated skirt. It was a nice foil to her hair which she piled on top of her head. She added the pearls, found the Italian slippers which had cost the earth and was putting things into her evening purse when Julius knocked and came in.

'That's nice.' He sounded like an old friend, easy and casual and she didn't understand why that annoyed her. He looked pretty good himself in a dark grey suit which fitted impeccably, but she hesitated to say so. She murmured a thank-you and went past him out of the room. Only she didn't quite get as far as that; he caught her gently and turned her round and kissed her. 'You really are rather a pretty girl,' he told her. And somehow that annoyed her even more.

They dined at their leisure while he told her something of his day. 'And tomorrow I must leave soon after nine and I'm afraid you'll have to have lunch on your own.' He frowned. 'I wonder if I should have come here before we married...it seemed a good idea.'

She said eagerly, 'Oh, but it was, it is. I'm not a lonely kind of person. I don't mind being on my own.' She paused. 'I miss Cuthbert...'

His smile was kind and understanding. 'I've two dogs at home; a golden retriever and a Boston Bull Terrier. I hope they'll make up for Cuthbert's loss. I miss them when I'm over here. You'll be able to see Cuthbert whenever we go to St Michael's—there's no reason why you shouldn't come with me; you can stay with your parents if you wish.'

'How often do you come?'

'Two or three times a year to lecture, quite frequently just for a day or two if I'm asked to give advice or operate.' He added, his eyes on her face. 'You won't be lonely, Josephine I promise you that.'

She looked up then. 'Oh, I know I shan't, especially if you'll let me go with you sometimes.'

He smiled. 'You will be able to look up your friends at St Michaels.'

He suggested a walk after dinner and when she joined him in her coat and a little cap, he asked, 'You will be warm enough?'

'Oh, yes! I've got my boots on too.' She sounded like a small child about to be given a treat. 'The shops look gorgeous. I love Christmas.'

'They'll miss you at home this year.'

She said soberly. 'Yes, though I hardly ever got home for Christmas Day because of being on duty you see. Do all your family meet at Christmas?'

'No—at the New Year. That's a very important day for us, the house bulges with children on Old Year's Day and the grown-ups see the New Year in and eat something very like your doughnuts and drink champagne. You may find Christmas very quiet. . .' He spoke casually, but his eyes beneath their heavy lids were watching her face.

'No, I shan't; you'll be there and we can have a tree, can't we? You do have Christmas trees?'

'Oh, yes,' he assured her gravely,' indeed we do. And there will be people dropping in for drinks and presents for everyone. Next year you will be there for St Nikolaas; more presents, though that's really for the children.'

They were walking through the lighted streets, stopping to look in windows and although Josephine had looked in the self same windows not six hours earlier it didn't matter in the least.

'Tomorrow I'll take you to the Castle Folk Museum, we can walk there if you feel like it. I should be back just after two o'clock and it's not far. We'll have tea in that place where the seats were pink plush and the cakes took your fancy.'

'That sounds marvellous. I'm going round the Minster again and there's the Treasurer's House to see. . .'

'Let's go there on the following day, and on the day after that they're giving a drinks party in the evening. Several people are anxious to meet you.' He looked down at her upturned face. 'Get yourself a pretty dress.' He added apropos of nothing, 'You looked so lovely in your wedding gown.'

She found herself short of breath. 'Oh, did I? I'm glad you liked it. I'll see if I can find something. It'll be an after six affair, I suppose? Something short?. . . Her thoughts happy and rather excited ran on: 'Green? No, I've got the green crêpe—a nice old rose. . .'

'Old rose it shall be. Let's go in here and have some coffee.'

They had breakfast together the next morning although it was still early and he had protested at her getting up.

'But I've been getting up early for years.' She reminded him. 'Besides, I've heaps of postcards to write.'

She wrote them in her room and then went out, intent this time on finding a dress. There were boutiques enough and several good department stores. She combed through them all, not finding what she wanted. But after a break for coffee she had success; a bow windowed shop with one or two outrageously priced dresses in the window, a small shop but once inside crammed with the kind of clothes every woman might dream of. In the quiet, grey carpeted salon she roamed from one rail to the next and found what she sought; old rose *crêpe de Chine* over taffeta with a plain neck line which would be just right for the pearls and long tight sleeves extravagently cuffed and buttoned with tiny satin covered buttons. It was a slim dress, cut by a masterly hand and worth every penny of its high price. Josephine paid for it without a qualm and went in search of a pair of shoes to go with it. She felt a little guilty as she ate her lunch; she had spent a great deal of money although, as she reminded herself, Julius had told her to do just that. On the way back to the hotel she bought several pairs of tights and some wildly expensive night cream, guaranteed to turn her into a raving beauty overnight and this regardless of the fact that she used soap and water on her already lovely face and, when she remembered, slapped on some cream or other.

Julius was sitting in the hotel lounge when she got back, reading *The Times* with the air of a man who had the rest of the day before him and nothing better to do. Certainly, she thought with some indignation, he didn't look like a man who was waiting for his wife.

She was of course unaware that he was sitting in front of a vast wall mirror which reflected the comings and goings of everyone through the foyer and that he had been sitting there for the last twenty minutes, so she was surprised to see him get up, fold his paper and come to meet her.

'I've kept you waiting?'

'No, my dear. I came back rather earlier than I had expected. You've had lunch?' His eyes fell on her parcels. 'And done some shopping? Would you like to rest for a little while or shall we go out?'

'Oh, out please.' She beamed at him, indignation forgotten. 'I'll just pop these in my room.'

He didn't answer that, merely took her packages from her and went over to the reception desk and handed them to the clerk. 'Want to powder your nose?' he enquired. 'I'll be here.'

She would have liked time to do her face and hair at length, as it was she dabbed her pretty nose, applied lipstick and whisked her hair into a state of tidiness; after all, he had surely got used to her appearance after several weeks of working with her at St Michael's. She had often looked a great deal worse. She hadn't worn a hat that morning and now she wondered if she should fetch a scarf and decided against it, suddenly impatient to be with Julius again.

They walked briskly to York Castle, paused to admire the ancient building built on top of the vast grass mound and gained the museum beyond it. It wasn't like a museum; Josephine, peering at perfect replicas of Victorian Parlours, Georgian dining rooms and humble cottages, was entranced. And the cobbled streets with their old-fashioned shops were not to be hurried over. It was getting dark when they emerged and she said contritely: 'Were you bored? I dawdled, but it was so fascinating. . .'

He took her arm. 'I wasn't bored.' And that was

true—he had been absorbed in watching her face, as excited and animated as a child's. 'Let's have tea.'

They walked back, past Ousegate and Parliament Street and into the narrow streets, ablaze with lights from the shop windows. 'There's a nice old-fashioned tea room,' Josephine suggested 'it's near that café with the pink plush. . .'

'Then we'll go there.' But on the way he stopped outside a narrow shop window, elegantly dressed with a brocade covered chair with a cashmere coat draped over it. 'Here first,' he said and urged her inside.

'A coat,' he asked blandly of the saleslady, 'a cashmere coat for my wife.'

Josephine and the saleslady stood and looked at him until the latter pulled herself together with a suave, 'Certainly. I'm sure that we have just the thing, sir. If I might know madam's size?'

Josephine blushed; the saleslady and Julius were both studying her and just for the moment she longed to be able to say 'ten: a slim boyish creature, able to wear anything and look gorgeous in it. 'I'm a fourteen,' she said in a challenging voice, and the saleslady went away with an underling in tow, leaving them for a moment alone.

Surprisingly, Julius bent and kissed her cheek. 'Wife dear, just remember this; I like you to be a size fourteen, don't ever be less; we match very nicely as we are. I'd look a fool with a beanpole on my arm, wouldn't I?' He grinned suddenly: 'Why do you suppose I married you?'

She didn't have time to answer, which was perhaps a good thing. A number of coats were displayed and she tried them on in turn, finally choosing a dark brown one and at the saleslady's suggestion a little fur cap to go with it. She hadn't dared ask the price; indeed she thought that Julius would be annoyed if she did. When they were out in the street however she thanked him warmly. 'It's super,' she assured him, 'I've never had anything as grand—I shall wear it. . .'

Julius laughed. 'That was the idea,' he observed. 'Now let's have tea.'

He was lecturing again the next day, in the morning, and she pottered around the shops for a while and then walked round the walls. It was a cold clear day, and she had the narrow path above the city very nearly to herself. It was quite an experience and she wished that Julius had been with her.

Mindful of his earlier arrival on the previous day, she took care to be back at the hotel well before two o'clock, only to find that he didn't turn up until half an hour later. His laconic, 'sorry I got held up,' was she realised all that she was going to know about it.

The Treasurer's House melted her slight peevishness; it was tucked away behind the Minster and now, in midwinter, there were no other visitors and only the Custodians sitting in its many rooms. They wandered around, taking their time, studying the paintings, marvelling that a house could be so comfortable three hundred years ago. The rooms were large and lofty and the staircase was ornately carved and the paintings were perfect of their kind, and upstairs the bedrooms looked as though they were lived in.

'Oh, I do like an old house,' declared Josephine as they regained the hall once again. 'Ours is old, of course, but it's only a small manor house—this is something quite different. How lovely to live in a place like this.'

Julius looked as if he was going to say something and then he changed his mind. 'It's a beautiful place,' he agreed, 'and in such splendid order.'

'It must cost a lot of money just to keep everything ticking over. . .'

'Oh, indeed.' He smiled a little, not looking at her. 'I like the clock pendulum hanging through a hole in the ceiling, one imagines it to be a giant of a timepiece and it's nothing of the sort.

They wandered to the door, paused to speak to the tweed clad lady sitting behind her table, and went out into the fast darkening afternoon.

'Tea?' said Julius, 'Let's go to that pink plush place again.'

And over tea he told her that he would be away for most of the next day. 'Sorry about it,' he said, not sounding at all sorry, and he added silkily, 'I did tell you that I would be working.'

She returned his thoughtful stare with a limpid one of her own. 'Well, of course you did. I've still got some more presents to buy.' She just managed not to ask what time he would be back. She might be his wife but just now and again she found herself feeling as though she were back on the ward being told to put up extra beds or be ready to take in an emergency.

'I'll be back around five o'clock,' he told her blandly. 'This party is around six-thirty and we'd better leave the Hotel around then. I'll have to shower and change, so shall we meet in the foyer then?'

'Suits me,' said Josephine with unexpected flippancy.

Their evening together had been pleasant, she reflected as she strolled around the shops once more. She had fibbed about buying presents; she had bought all she wanted to buy but on no account must he guess that she had nothing to do with her day. There were several museums still but she wasn't much interested in Roman remains and railways, so she spent a long time over coffee and then went to Marks and Spencer looking carefully at every counter and happily remembering that she hadn't bought anything for Mrs Bagg. It took upwards of half an hour to find something suitable; Mrs Bagg was a law unto herself clotheswise, favouring jumble sales and anything the ladies she worked for offered her. Josephine settled finally for a sensible cardigan; Mrs Bagg was keen on those and always wore one over her cotton pinny when she came to clean. She added a box of soaps and then went in search of lunch.

The afternoon dragged, she went back to the hotel, had tea in the lounge and went upstairs, glad that at last she could start getting ready for the evening. There was plenty of time and she took pains; the end result was stunning; the pink dress was flattering and fitted where it should and her hair went up with no trouble at all. She took a final look at herself in the long glass, and since there was no sign of Julius, picked up her fur coat and went down to the lounge.

Her entry caused a number of heads to turn, but she avoided the stares and went to sit down in one of the window seats, hardly noticing the interest she had stirred up. Presently though, one of the men sitting at the bar at the farther end of the lounge walked across to her.

She refused his perfectly polite offer of a drink and after a moment he went back again and a minute later Julius came in. He was still in his overcoat and carrying a brief case and she saw that he was in one of his cool and distant moods.

He didn't bother with a greeting. 'I expected you to be in your room,' he told her coldly, 'not down here waiting to be picked up. . .'

She lost her breath at that; she itched to slap his handsome, angry face, but instead she got to her feet and went past him and upstairs to her room. He was just behind her but she shut the door in his face, turned the key and then locked the door to the bathroom. She wasn't going to cry, she told herself savagely, he wasn't worth it. How dared he, oh, how dared he?'

If she had expected him to rattle the door handles or try and talk to her through the door, she was mistaken. She heard the shower being turned on and ten minutes later his voice, cool and quiet, 'Open the door, Josephine.'

It would have given her the greatest satisfaction

to have bawled, 'I won't,' at him, but presumably they would still have to go to this party. She opened it.

He stood in front of her impeccably turned out, his face expressionless. 'I'm sorry,' he said, and somehow made nonsense of the words, 'I have upset you, and I apologise.'

'But why?'

He said, suddenly savage: 'Oh, nothing of importance. Are you ready? And then, 'I do hope you will forgive me?'

'Yes, of course. I expect you were tired.' She added gently 'But next time I shall slap your face, Julius.'

'There won't be a next time. Shall we go?'

He might have a bad temper but she couldn't fault his manners. He treated her to a polite conversation as they drove to Leeds and once they were there, behaved exactly as a newly married man would be expected to behave.

She was an instant success; rage had heightened her colour and given her grey eyes a sparkle and the pink dress made her more beautiful than ever. She accepted compliments gracefully, listened gravely to several of the more elderly learned gentlemen present, smiled kindly at the younger ones and gossiped with the wives while she sipped frugally at her sherry and wondered about dinner. The party showed no signs of breaking up and she was very hungry.

People started to go at last, stopping for a final chat, issuing invitations for the following trip Julius would take to England, exchanging messages with each other. They were in the car finally, driving back to York, exchanging polite small talk until they were in the bar once more, drinking what was for Josephine one sherry too many before they had dinner. She realised that she had had enough already and at any moment now she might allow her tongue full rein. Actually, she found that she couldn't care less; her eyes still sparkled, what with sherry and rage, and her colour had, if anything, become even more spectacular.

Most of the occupants of the bar watched them go into the restaurant, they made a splendid pair.

Over their dinner Julius asked her with cool politeness if she would mind if they spent a night in London on their way back. 'We'll go to your parents, of course, but perhaps we might arrive for lunch and leave in the evening? I wanted to see Mr Bull before we go back home.'

Mr Bull had been at their wedding, but there had been no chance to talk shop; she realised that; probably they had some knotty surgical problem they wished to unravel together. She agreed, with a cool politeness to match his, that she didn't mind in the least.

They were to leave in the morning, it gave her a good reason not to linger too long over their coffee. It had been a pleasant evening but they had quarrelled: well, not exactly that perhaps because she was vague as to why he had been so angry. If a girl—a married woman—couldn't sit in a hotel bar by herself then it was a poor show. It crossed her mind that to enter a bar on her own was something she wouldn't have thought of doing in the ordinary way. She had wanted Julius to see her in the new pink dress the minute he had returned. And he hadn't even noticed it. . .

He walked with her to the stairs and wished her good night and then took her hand. 'Friends?' he asked, no longer coldly polite. 'Such a waste of time to treat each other like this. It's the kind of thing one expects young lovers to do; hate each other and then love each other more than ever before.'

'I don't hate you,' Josephine told him clearly and stared up at him as though she had never seen him before. Thoughts crowded her head, a fearful jumble which she wished very much to make clear to him, but before she could utter a sound a bellboy came to fetch him to the telephone. He bade her good night, excused himself and crossed the foyer away from her. She watched him go. Just as well, she told herself, craning her neck to see the last of his broad back; he hadn't married her for love, he had made that clear, had he not? He wouldn't be any too pleased if she told him that even if she hadn't loved him when they married, she did now. The knowledge had struck her with the suddenness of a thunderbolt and it was a very good thing that she had a few hours alone in which to pull herself together. It was a situation which needed thinking about.

CHAPTER EIGHT

JOSEPHINE undressed slowly, pottering round the room, packing after a fashion, stopping to sit on the bed and do nothing, trying to think clearly. Every time she tried to do this she was frustrated because she thought about Julius instead. When had she fallen in love with him? she asked herself, and why had she only discovered it now, and how marvellous it would be if he were to fall in love with her.

But this, she told herself at once, was foolish thinking; if he had loved her he would have said so when he had asked her to marry him. She recalled everything he had said and had to admit that there had never been even a suspicion of that, and this evening he had looked at her as though he had wanted to shake her till her teeth rattled. . .

She rammed the remainder of her clothes into her case, got into bed and turned off the light. This, she told herself once more, needed a clear brain and sensible thinking; it was no good feeling sorry for herself and wishing the impossible. Sound advice which, however, didn't stop her burying her face in the pillow and crying her eyes out.

She woke in the small hours, the time when problems doubled their size, gloomy thoughts became even more gloomy and rational thought

171

became hopelessly entangled with fantasy. It was early morning, and the traffic had started on a new day when she slept again, hopelessly muddled although one resolution had emerged from the chaos; Julius must never know.

Pointless, as it turned out; a quick look at her face at breakfast was enough to appraise him of the fact that her eyelids were puffy and still a trifle pink and that there were shadows under her eyes. His, 'What's the matter, Josephine?' was uttered casually but with a warm sympathy which almost betrayed her into an impetuous speech. She paused, her fork half way to her mouth. 'Nothing—nothing at all.' She was aware that she had sounded too emphatic and added lamely: 'I didn't sleep very well—all the excitement of the party, I expect.'

He agreed, his voice dry, his eyes still searching her face. 'The weather forecast is not good, I think it will be as well if we leave soon after breakfast. I'll pick up the MI and then cross over on to the M6 so to the M5 and turn off at Gloucester. That should get us to your parents in the early afternoon. Shall I give your mother a ring? Would she give us a meal in the early evening; we could leave about eight o'clock and be in town well before midnight?'

It sounded strenuous but she agreed without a murmur. The Bentley could keep up a steady seventy for hours on end and Julius was a splendid driver. She finished her breakfast and went upstairs to close her case and presently emerged very neat and serene, to wait composedly while

Julius saw that their luggage was brought down and put into the car. He settled her beside him, remarking that her mother would be delighted to see them whenever they arrived and without more ado took the car gently through the narrow streets.

He had been right about the weather. Josephine, surveying the slate grey skies all round them, hoped that the rain would hold off, although she thought it unlikely that it would make any difference to Julius's plan.

He drove steadily and once on the MI sent the needle up to seventy and kept it there. It was monotonous on the motorway and although it was still dry the sky hung heavily and low above them. They didn't talk much and presently Josephine gave up. Julius's silence was friendly, but he obviously didn't want to talk—a surgical problem, perhaps, to be discussed with Mr Bull before they left for Holland. Come to think of it, she had problems of her own.

They had left the MI and turned on to the M6 when he asked: 'Like to stop for ten minutes? Coffee and a sandwich? Can you hold out without lunch? It will snow before dark I think and I'd like to get to Ridge Giffard. We've made good time; we'll cut across through Warwick to Tewksbury, go down the M3 and turn off on to the Motorway as far as Chippenham and then down the A350.'

She wondered if he knew his way round his own country as well as he could find his way round here. How had he discovered that at this time of year the roman roads would be as fast as a Motorway with almost no traffic? 'Yes, I'd like to stop and ten minutes is enough time, thanks. I'm not hungry and Mother is sure to have a splendid meal for us. Do you mean to go on to London this evening whatever the weather?'

A service station sprawled ahead of them, he slowed the car and parked before he answered her. 'Yes—bad weather won't bother you?'

'Me, heavens no.' She skipped out and they went inside into the stuffy warmth. Just over ten minutes later they were getting back into the car. The coffee had been hot and weak and the sandwiches had been wrapped by a fiendish hand in too tight cling-film and they had laughed about it so that just for a few minutes she had a glimpse of a different Julius. But once in the car, he reverted to a silence broken only occasionally by a query as to her comfort or a comment upon the road or the weather. She went back to her thoughts, and being young and sensible, she found herself looking forward to the future; he liked her, even when he was coolly polite and absorbed she still knew he liked her, she thought that he was proud of her; she wasn't conceited but she knew that she was pretty and that people liked her, she would make him a good wife, she understood the irregular hours he might keep, she could run a house and cook and entertain his friends; he would never need to be ashamed of her. And they liked the same things. She became so lost in thought that she started when he said quietly: 'There's the A350—not long now and it's beginning to snow.'

She peered from the window into the rapidly

darkening outside. 'So it is—I didn't notice. . .'

'Were you very far away?' He wanted to know.

'Yes!' In cloud cuckoo land, she added silently, solving all my problems without difficulty. 'This is a comfy car. Aren't you tired?'

He sounded surprised. 'Lord no, I enjoy driving, it gives me time to think.'

She said matter-of-factly: 'About your patients.' She wasn't looking at him and she didn't see his slow smile, only heard him agree gravely.

There was almost no traffic and the road ran straight and empty for long stretches and they were in her own part of the world now. Daylight had almost gone and the snow was falling steadily but not too thickly.

'Snow for Christmas,' said Josephine.

'Very likely, if it freezes we will be able to skate.'

'I've only tried that once or twice, I don't think I'll be much good. . .'

'There is a small pond close to the house, I'll teach you, it's easy enough once you've got your balance.'

They were through Warminster and presently turned into a side road, narrow and high hedged and he slowed the car.

'This is where we met for the first time,' he said abruptly. 'You gave me the sharp edge of your tongue.'

'Oh, I did, I can't think why, only you looked at me as though—as though you couldn't bear the sight of me.'

'Shock,' said Julius gravely, 'causes people to behave in the strangest way.'

She had no chance to ask him what on earth he meant for they were at the front door, and her Mother had opened it, letting the light stream out to welcome them.

Lovely to be home, thought Josephine, embracing her parent and on top of that thought: regret that the journey was over, just sitting beside Julius had been bliss. She mustn't allow her mind to dwell on that.

They were all home for Christmas, Natalie and Mike and her father back from his afternoon rounds and Cuthbert weaving himself ponderously in and out of everyone's legs. They were swept into the sitting room and settled before the fire and given tea while everyone talked at once. Josephine, sitting next to her Mother, assured her that she was happy, that York had been marvellous and that she was looking forward to her new home. 'And we'll be over directly after New Year! Julius said so.'

Mrs Dowling glanced across to where her son-in-law was sitting talking to her husband. He turned his head and smiled at her and she said in a tone of deep satisfaction: 'He'll be a splendid husband, Jo.'

Josephine agreed. 'We've got some presents in the boot,' she said rather quickly, not wanting to enlarge upon Julius's husbandly qualities. 'I'll get him to bring them in. We have to leave about half past eight, he's got to be in town tonight ready for Mr Bull early in the morning.'

'In that case I'll go and look at that joint in the oven,' declared Mrs Dowling.

The presents were brought in presently and those from the family put into the boot, to be opened on Christmas Day and not before, and soon they all sat down to one of Mrs Dowlings beautifully cooked meals; Spinach soup, roast pork and apple sauce, baked potatoes and celery and sprouts, and since they would be apart for Christmas, one of her Christmas puddings. Another half hour round the fire with their coffee and it was time to go. Just for a moment the two of them were together in the general melée and Julius said with sudden urgency, 'Josephine, there's something. . .'

She wasn't to know what it was; the family surged round them once more admiring the fur coat, begging them to drive carefully, to 'phone when they arrived and to have a happy Christmas. They were escorted to the door to find that it had stopped snowing and the moon shining down on a thin blanket of white was brilliant, a fairytale world. They began a round of goodbyes and when it was Mrs Dowling's turn Julius kissed her with a warmth which made her eyes sparkle. Josephine was standing beside them, he kissed her too, not his usual brief salute on one cheek but quick and hard on her surprised mouth.

The drove away from the cheerful lights of the house, talking at first and then submitting to a companionable silence. The roads were fairly empty and the moon lighted the quiet countryside, even the motorway when they reached it, looked mysterious and very beautiful. Josephine sat quietly; she didn't want to think, just to enjoy the happiness of sitting by Julius. Presently she went to sleep; she didn't hear Julius when he said quietly, 'Josephine I must talk to you. . .'

He glanced at her sleeping face and he looked ahead again, his face expressionless. She didn't wake until they were at the flat, sitting up suddenly and very straight. 'We're never here already, I've been asleep,' she told him unnecessarily, and then, 'What's the time?'

'Almost eleven o'clock. I'll see you in and bring in the luggage and then put the car away. Mrs Twigg will have left coffee and some food. Your room is the third door on the left.'

They went up together to find the flat cosily warm and lighted. Julius went through it, switching on more lights, pointing out the kitchen and thrusting open her bedroom door. 'Make yourself at home, my dear, I shan't be long.' His voice was placid and unhurried and he smiled at her. 'Tired?'

'No—yes, but I've enjoyed every minute of the day,' she declared.

When he had gone again she took off her outdoor things, taking no more than a hasty glance at her room and then she went to the kitchen. Small, but so well planned that there seemed to be room for everything any housewife might need, with the coffee percolator waiting for her and a note on the table to say that a light supper was in the fridge—paper thin sandwiches, little meat patties, vol-au-vents and sausage rolls. A tray with cutlery and cloth and napkins too, was ready on the dresser and there was soup on the Aga.

Josephine busied herself with the meal and by the time Julius came into the room, the soup was simmering and the coffee bubbling.

'A gorgeous little spread,' she told him happily. 'Shall I take it all through to the dining room?'

'Lord no. I'll get the table ready and get us drinks and you can get the food. What would you like? A weak gin and tonic? I know you don't drink it usually, but anything else might keep you awake.'

She nodded happily and stirred her soup, smiling to herself, remembering what a different man Julius was on the wards to this relaxed man pottering around his flat. Briefly she wondered what it was that he had wanted to tell her so urgently at her home; whatever it was couldn't have been very important for he hadn't said any more about it and he had had opportunity enough in the car as they drove up.

They had their drinks as they got their small meal together and presently sat down to eat it, and when Josephine would have cleared the table and washed the dishes she was told firmly that Mrs Twigg would see to all that in the morning and that she was to go to bed at once. So she put up her sleepy face for his brief kiss and went to her room. Julius had left the bedside lights on and it looked invitingly cosy. She unpacked her night things and went to run a bath and then lay in it half asleep while she went over her day. What a lot one could pack into twenty-four hours, she mused, even falling in love. . . She felt the tears crowd her throat and got out of the bath, telling herself fiercely that Julius must have given her a very large gin and tonic to make her so weepy. She got into bed, convinced that she wouldn't sleep and went out like a light; when she opened her eyes it was to find Mrs Twigg standing by the bed with a tray of early morning tea. There was a note on it from Julius, telling her in a few businesslike sentences that he would be back about tea time. There was a key on the tray too, in case she wanted to go out while he was away.

She drank her tea, showered and dressed and ate the breakfast Mrs Twigg had cooked so perfectly and then, because she felt at a loss, she told the housekeeper that she would be out to lunch, put the key in her handbag donned the fur coat and little hat against the decidedly wintery weather and went out.

Christmas was so near now that the shops were crowded and so were the pavements. She wandered along, finally making her way to Harrods and spent a long time there, buying a lipstick she didn't really need, tights because they always came in handy, and finally a present for Julius.

No easy choice this. He had, as far as she could discover, everything. She spent a long time poring over ties; his taste was quiet; he loved silk in rich subdued colours, and there was an abundance of choice. She finally chose two, costing almost as much as she would have spent on a dress. Then pleased with her purchases she wandered around until she found something else; a slim pocket book, beautifully bound in calf and with his initials in gold. The salesman assured her that he could have them ready for her in a couple of hours. She wandered off again to have coffee and potter round the various departments. She would have liked to have gone to St Michael's but Julius might have thought that she was spying on him. . .

She had an early lunch, fetched the pocket book and walked back to the flat. It was still early afternoon, she had several hours to fill in before Julius would be back. She remembered then that he hadn't said when they would be going to Holland. She hadn't asked either, she let herself into the flat to find Mrs Twigg busy in the kitchen. 'Just clearing up, as you might say, Madam,' she was told. 'I'll get tea for four o'clock if that suits you? Mr van Tacx said he'd be back by then. Just leave everything; I'll be in to clear away in the morning as usual.'

It seemed as though they would be leaving sometime in the evening. Josephine took off her outdoor things and settled down in the sitting room with a book. She didn't read it, she had too much to think about. But her usual common sense seemed to have deserted her; she sat day dreaming and never heard the flat door open or the quiet voices until Julius walked into the room with Mr Bull ahead of him.

Josephine leapt from her chair, still not quite back in the world and feeling guilty about it, but Mr Bull hadn't noticed; he surged forward gave her a smacking kiss, told her that she looked as pretty as a picture and observed in tones of satisfaction that being married suited her.

'Not that we don't miss you on the ward. My word, we do. Joan's very good but I can see that before long she and Matt are going to make a match of it and then heaven help us all.'

Josephine laughed. 'Don't be so pessimistic,' she begged him, 'you'll stay for tea?' She smiled at Julius. 'Had a busy day?' she asked.

'Yes, Josephine, did I forget to tell you that we're going over to Holland this evening?'

'Well, yes, you did.' She spoke lightly for the benefit of Mr Bull, 'but I thought that perhaps we might be—I'm ready to leave whenever you want to.' She laughed. 'Tea first?'

He came across the room and dropped a kiss on her cheek and she pinkened and Mr Bull made matters worse by exclaiming: 'Young love,' and still worse, 'Don't mind me.'

'I'll just see about tea,' said Josephine and escaped.

There was nothing to see about, of course, Mrs Twigg had the whole business in hand, all that Josephine had to do was to sit at the small Pembroke table and hand the tea and press her companions to eat Mrs Twigg's delicious little sandwiches and cakes.

Mr Bull went presently, full of Christmas good wishes and the reminder that he would be seeing Julius in the new year. It seemed very quiet after he had left. It was Julius who broke the silence with an enquiry as to how she had spent her day.

'Oh, pottering round,' she told him cheerfully, 'last minute presents and so on. Mrs Twigg's still here. . .'

'She'll stay until we go,' he glanced at his watch. 'Can you be ready in an hour? We'll get the night ferry from Harwich. Do you want to 'phone your mother before we leave?'

'Phoning home was a lengthy business because everyone wanted a word with her and then Julius took the receiver from her just as she was about to hang up and talked to her mother. He was sitting on the arm of one of the chairs, swinging a leg and watching her, laughing at something her mother had said. 'We'll be over during the first week of January,' he said finally, 'we'll 'phone when we get home.'

He put the receiver down, still watching Josephine. He wasn't laughing any more. 'We have to talk. . .' He stopped as there was a knock on the door and Mrs Twigg came in to ask for instructions as to what they wanted of her while they were away and when would they be back and could Mrs van Tacx come to the kitchen and decide what might be needed to stock the freezer against their return. Julius answered her patiently and when he'd finished Josephine went to the kitchen with the housekeeper. The list took longer than she had expected, and Mrs Twigg, a meticulous and house proud woman liked to discuss each and every item. By the time they had finished an hour or more had gone by and when she went back to the sitting room, Julius told her that he wanted to leave within twenty minutes.

'You were going to tell me something?'

He shook his head. 'Not enough time,' he said

impassively. 'Go and put on your coat and let me have the cases.'

They talked about all manner of things on their way to the Ferry, but none of them personal. Indeed, Josephine had the feeling that he was deliberately keeping it that way. They dined on board and since they would arrive early in the morning, she was advised to go early to bed.

She had fancied to go on deck with Julius and watch the ship leave. Perhaps there, with no one much around, he would tell her whatever it was he thought that she should know, but he had made no such suggestion. She went down to her comfortable cabin, took her time about getting ready for bed, and finally got into her narrow bunk and went to sleep.

The Hoek looked bleak in the still early morning and it was dark as they disembarked after a quick breakfast of coffee and rolls, but the Customs sheds were as bright as day and bustling with any number of persons hurrying to and fro in a purposeful manner. Josephine gazed around her with interest, keeping close to Julius while they and the car were processed through the formalities and into the street outside.

'Home for breakfast,' Julius told her cheerfully, as they left the town behind them and joined the motorway. 'Very dull,' explained Julius, 'but it's quick from here.'

Josephine, usually sensible and calm, suddenly felt sick with nervousness. 'Is your home in Leiden?' she asked and wished that she had made it her business to find out more about it before this.

'No, in a village just outside. There is a lake close by and some woods. It's a very small village and off the main road, but it's only ten minutes into Leiden with the car. All the family are coming to dinner this evening but you shall have the rest of the day to sleep if you want to. A friend of mine will be there too—he has an English wife and they haven't been married long—she's just had their second child. I think you'll like her. They live near Hilversum, no distance from us.'

They were approaching Leiden and Julius turned off the motorway and drove into the narrow streets of the town. It was still too early for many people to be about and Josephine looked her fill as they passed the old gabled houses and the Town Hall. Here was Holland just as she had imagined it from seeing Pieter de Hoog and van Meer and all the rest of the old masters. 'Oh, it's simply splendid,' she declared, 'are the houses old inside like the paintings?'

'Most of them, carefully restored, of course.'

They were out of the town now and going along a country road with wide frost covered fields on either side, but presently Julius turned off into a narrow lane with trees on either side bordering a small canal. The lane curved and Josephine could see the dim outline of houses ahead of them.

'The village,' said Julius and slowed the car to go round the cobbled square with its church in the centre. He sent the car round another corner and in a hundred yards or so turned in between two massive gate posts. There was a short drive beyond that opened into a wide gravel sweep before the house.

Josephine drew a breath of surprise. It was more than a house, it was a solid country gentleman's residence, eighteenth century, she guessed, red brick, heavily ornamented with plasterwork, its large windows set in precise rows across it's dignified face. It had a gabled roof and circular steps leading to its outside front door.

Julius had stopped the car and sat looking at her. She said at length, 'This is your home. . .?'

'Our home,' he corrected her. 'Come inside, my dear, and be welcomed.'

They got out and he took her arm and as they mounted the steps together the door was opened by tall, thin elderly man with a bald head and a whiskered face. Julius shook his hand and clapped him on the shoulder and introduced him. 'This is Borren; he has been with the family ever since I can remember and before that.'

Borren shook hands and surprised her by speaking English. Heavily accented but understandable. She beamed at him and urged gently forward by Julius went into the square vestibule and beyond it into the hall.

There were several persons in it; they chorused a greeting and Julius said something which made them laugh before taking her arm again and introducing them. 'Borren's wife,' he explained, 'and the housekeeper'. A cheerfully smiling little woman she sensed that she would like, and after her two young women, Else and Anna, and a middle aged woman who came in from the village each day to help in the house, and lastly an old man and a teenage boy—Wim the gardener and his assistant Hans.

'And that's all of us,' Julius observed as she shook the last hand. 'Welcome to our home, my dear.' He bent and kissed her and everyone clapped.

Josephine blushed, wondering if he had kissed her because it was the custom or because he had wanted to. The latter, she hoped, for she had kissed him back with unguarded warmth.

'Very nice,' said Julius, 'we should do that more often.'

She didn't need to answer that because *Mevrouw* Borren trotted forward to say something to him, beaming at them both. 'Breakfast,' said Julius. 'Would you like to go to your room first?' He smiled at her, a nice friendly smile. 'Ten minutes?'

Mevrouw Borren led the way up the wide oak staircase at the back of the square hall, along a gallery and threw open double doors on to a large room at the front of the house. Josephine's first impression was of light; even on this winter morning the vast windows and the high ceiling gave the room a bright and airy appearance, that coupled with the cream carpet underfoot, the Hepplewhite bed and dressing table and the cream and pink curtains and bedspread, made the whole place a delight. There was a balcony running the whole length of one wall and a bathroom leading from one side. On the other wall there were two doors, *Mevrouw* Borren opened them in turn; a clothes closet and a smaller bedroom. Julius's, Josephine supposed.

The housekeeper smiled and nodded and left her, and Josephine tidied herself and took another quick survey of her room. There were easy chairs each side of a small open fire; a luxury she had never expected to see, and a magnificent mahogany tall boy against one wall; and there were flowers on the bedside tables as well as books and magazines. She was used to living in some comfort in her parent's house, but this was luxury. She went downstairs once again, taking her time, inspecting the portraits on the walls. If they were anything to go by, Julius had inherited the features of every ancestor he ever had. The clothes had changed, that was all.

She paused on the bottom step and Julius came and opened one of the doors in the hall and came towards her. 'Hungry?' he wanted to know. 'And you must be tired. I'll have to go into Leiden after breakfast, so why don't you have a nap? I'll be back sometime in the afternoon and we can go round the house before the family arrive.'

She agreed happily enough and together they ate the rolls and coffee Borren served them, and while they ate, Josephine took a look at the dining room. Panelled walls, painted white, a misty green ceiling heavily decorated with plasterwork, a circular table of some size and a vast side table. There were flowers everywhere and the carpets and curtains were a rich tawny colour so that the room glowed.

'Like it?' asked Julius.

'Very much, my bedroom is super too.' She added hesitantly 'Must you really go to Leiden?'

'Afraid so. We don't see much of each other do we, Josephine?'

'No, but it won't always be like this, will it? I mean you'll be home each day—you do live here. . .'

His stare disconcerted her. 'You'll be happy here?'

'Oh, yes'. Of course she would be happy; just to be in the same house as he was, sit with him at table, be home to welcome him when he got back after a day's work. Not completely happy, perhaps, but it would have to do to go on with.

'Do I have to dress up for this evening?' she wanted to know.

'Oh, I think so.' He got up and came round the table and bent to kiss her cheek. 'No regrets, my dear?'

She shook her head. 'None,' she said and smiled at him as he left the room.

It was still not mid-morning; she decided to take Julius's advice and go to bed. She found Borren and told him and went up to her room and lost no time in climbing into her bed. She was asleep within minutes and only wakened when *Mevrouw* Borren came into her room with her lunch on a tray. A delicious meal which she ate, still sleepy, and then curled up again and slept. But not for long; she was up and dressed and wandering round a rather grand room which she supposed was the drawing room when Julius got back.

'Had a good sleep?' He wanted to know. 'Borren looked after you?'

'Oh, yes thank you. He was hovering when I came downstairs but I thought it would be fun to look round on my own, you don't mind?'

'My dear girl, this is your home, of course I don't mind. How far have you got?'

She laughed a little. 'Halfway round this room—there's such a lot to look at.'

And indeed there was; a large room, with tall windows at one end draped in old rose velvet and white painted walls picked out with gilding and hung with portraits and landscapes. The furniture was a thoughtful mixture of antiques and modern sofas and armchairs, with a great bowfronted cabinet, along one wall, displaying silver and china. The opposite wall was largely taken up by an enormous chimney piece with a gleaming hood above it and a splendid fire burning. She had been standing on tiptoe, trying to examine a painting to one side of it when Julius had come into the room, now she sat down on a crinoline chair and enquired after his day.

'Oh, nothing much,' he told her and stretched out in a vast wing chair opposite her. 'Just getting some idea of the work waiting: I'll have to get as much done before Christmas as I can.'

'I asked Borren to bring the tea here, is that all right?' She suddenly felt shy of him, sitting there as though they had been sitting comfortably together for years. 'There's a dog somewhere—I haven't seen him yet.'

'That'll be Charlie. Borren fetched him from the

vet's while you were asleep. I expect he thought it best to wait until I was home before he was introduced. He's not dangerous; only large.'

Borren came in then with the tea tray and following him came a Great Dane, pacing in a stately manner until he saw Julius, when he skidded across the room to rear up on his hind legs and greet him.

'Oh, he is nice,' cried Josephine, 'I do hope he'll like me.'

It seemed as if he would; introduced he wagged his tail, licked her hand gently and then sat and gazed at her with his tongue hanging out.

Presently he went to sit at his master's feet, still gazing at her, eyes half shut, listening to their quiet talk.

'You said two dogs,' she reminded him.

'My father's got the other one—he'll bring him over later.'

Afterwards, when they had had their tea, they went round the house together with Charlie padding along beside them; a brief inspection of the dining room, where the two girls were already getting the table ready for dinner, a longer look at the library opening out of it, and then through a door into a covered terrace running across the back of the house. They went from here through french windows into a pleasant, much smaller room, where Julius, told her she might prefer to sit. Indeed it was very much to her taste, with a cosy fire burning in it's old fashioned steel grate and heavy brocade curtains drawn against the dark. There was a door in the opposite wall, opening on to a short arched passage with a door at the end. 'My study,' said Julius, and opened the door just sufficiently for her to get a glimpse of a solid desk and leather chairs. 'We'll leave the kitchen until later, shall we, *Mevrouw* Borren won't want us there while she is cooking.'

Upstairs she was led from one room to another, all equally beautiful with their plaster ceilings ornately decorated with swags of fruit and flowers, softly carpeted and furnished with antiques lovingly polished.

'Your family have lived here for a long time?'

'Two hundred and thirty years.' He was leaning against a closet door, his hands in his pockets, watching her as she bent to smooth the needlework tapestry in a small chair. 'The van Tacx who built it made a fortune in the East Indies. Did I ever tell you that I am a rich man, Josephine?'

She straightened up to look at him. 'No, though I thought you might be comfortably off—I mean the Bentley and my fur coat and those pearls.' Her hand went to her throat to touch them lightly. 'You're not very rich are you?'

'Oh, yes, I am. Do you mind?'

'No, I don't suppose so.' She smiled suddenly. 'It wouldn't make any difference if I did, would it?'

'None whatever,' he said coolly. 'We had better go and change—the family will be here in an hour. I'll take Charlie for a quick run first. Come down when you are ready, I'll be in the drawing room.'

She went past him and started down the staircase. 'I love this house,' she assured him, and then diffidently, 'Julius, may I just telephone my mother?'

'Of course, whenever you like. I did ring this morning from the hospital, just to let them know that we'd arrived safely.'

She thanked Julius warmly, had a brief talk with her mother and went to dress. The occasion, she felt, was an important one; she chose a silver grey taffeta, with a long skirt, a scooped out neckline and extravagently puffed sleeves. She hadn't been quite sure about it when she had tried it on, but now, looking at her reflection in the pier glass, she felt satisfied. It matched her eyes and highlighted her hair. She clasped the pearls around her throat, put the rose diamonds on her fingers and went downstairs.

Julius was already in the drawing room, standing with one elegantly shod foot on the massive fender, a glass in his hand. She thought rather wildly as she went in that if she hadn't been head over heels in love with him, she would be now. He put his glass down and came over to meet her.

'Oh, very nice,' he observed, 'very nice indeed.' He took her hands and held her arms wide and studied her slowly. 'Perfect.' He let go of her hands and took a box from a pocket. 'Will you wear these? They were my mother's.'

Earrings, pearl drops hanging from diamond clusters, flashing fire as she took them in her hand. 'They are exquisite. Thank-you, Julius.' She wanted to fling herself at him and kiss him but thought he might not like that. Instead she went to a tall mirror and put them on, turning this way and that to catch their sparkle. He had come to stand behind her, looking at her in the mirror and she found that she couldn't take her eyes away from him.

He smiled slowly. 'Josephine, I have wanted to say something to you and each time I was prevented; once you were asleep. . .I think that I should have said it long ago, but perhaps it is not too late, I believe not. . .'

There was a faint commotion in the hall and several cheerful voices all talking at once. Julius's face became impassive. 'It seems I am to be interrupted once more.' He turned away. 'I have a strong feeling of sympathy for your Mr Browning; did he not complain; "Never the time and the place and the loved one altogether"?'

He was at the door as he spoke and she wasn't sure that she had heard him aright. She said urgently, 'Julius. . .' but the door opened and the van Tacx family came in.

CHAPTER NINE

BOTH Julius and Josephine were instantly surrounded; his father, his brothers and sisters and a
scattering of Aunts and Uncles, all rather grand,
especially the elderly ladies of the party, well cor-
seted and wearing discreetly fabulous jewellery on
their formidable bosoms.

Josephine was introduced, kissed, and
exclaimed over in the kindest possible way. Even
so, she was grateful for Julius's towering presence
beside her. Some ten minutes later the last of the
guests arrived. They stood for a moment in the
doorway and Julius said, 'Ah, the van Diederijks,'
and took her arm and went to meet them.
'Josephine, this is Euphemia and this is Tane.' He
kissed Euphemia and shook his friend's hand and
Josephine had time to take stock of Euphemia;
almost as tall as herself, rather plump with large
quantities of dark hair and a charming face.

They smiled at each other as they shook hands
and Euphemia said: 'I know all about you—Julius
came to see us weeks ago and described you down
to the last eyelash. I do so hope we'll be friends.
Do you like babies?'

'Oh, yes.'

'Good—we've got two already. Little Tane,
he's two and a bit and Marijke, she's almost three
months. You must come and see them.'

They all joined the rest of the guests, drank their sherry and then went in to dinner, and in the pleasant little bustle of everyone finding where they were to sit, Josephine had time to take stock of Tane. He was older than Julius, but only a year or so with fair, silvery hair and blue eyes, he was good looking and his voice was pleasant. She noted with pleasure not unmixed with envy that as far as he was concerned there was no one else in the room except his Euphemia. She was going to like them both.

Dinner was superb; *Mevrouw* Borren obviously excelled as a cook; sorrel soup, served in very fine old Delft plates, followed by hot salmon paté with side salads and then raised game pie accompanied by game chips and braised celery, tiny green peas and aubergines. All these rounded off by ice creams, sorbets and Pavlova Cake. Even for a special occasion such as this, Josephine found it magnificent; the table sparkled with silver and glass and they drank champagne, and Julius sitting opposite her at the head of the table, smiled and raised his glass to her in a silent toast. It was at the end of dinner that old *Mijnheer* van Tacx got to his feet to toast his son and daughter-in-law and after Julius had made a brief speech in reply, several members of the family got up and made speeches in their turn so that the evening was well advanced by the time they all went back to the drawing-room for coffee. Josephine found herself between two formidable aunts, both bent on cross examining her in a kindly way and she wished she hadn't drunk quite so much champagne at dinner.

She caught Julius's eye and smiled at him with unconscious appeal and he came across the room to stand beside her and say lightly: 'My darling, *Oom* Huib wants to talk to you, if *Tante* Beatrix and *Tante* Wilhelmenia can spare you for a few moments?'

Oom Huib was a dear old man, his English pedantic and almost without accent, and presently they were joined by Julius's father, and she sat between the two of them, feeling happy, sensing that they both liked her and welcomed her into the family. As indeed they all had. The aunts looked fierce but they were kindness itself. Listening to the babble of voices around her, she decided that the first thing to do was to learn to speak Dutch.

Presently Euphemia came over and the two old gentlemen went to join other members of the family observing that they might like a chance to get to know each other.

'You're enjoying it?' Euphemia sounded a little anxious. 'Julius has such a large family, and you only arrived this morning didn't you?'

'I had a sleep for most of the day,' smiled Josephine.

'I suppose Julius will be working flat out now until Christmas. You'll be here? So shall we, but we'll go to England in the New Year. Tane goes over a lot and we go with him. We've a house—it used to be my home—it's close to Chobham and Tane goes to and fro each day. We have my brothers to stay there and my sister and her family. Julius has a flat in London, hasn't he?' She smiled warmly, 'I hope you'll be very happy—well I know you will—how could you help it with someone as nice as Julius.' She got up. 'People are beginning to leave. May I 'phone you one day soon and we'll meet?'

'I'd like that very much and I'd like to see the babies too.'

It took quite some time to bid everyone goodbye, and make arrangements to meet in the future, exchange all the farewell courtesies; the house seemed very quiet when the last guest had gone. Josephine went slowly back to the drawing-room while Borren bolted the doors and Julius stayed to say something to him. She turned to him as he reached her: 'Julius, I'd like to thank *Mevrouw* Borren; do you think I might go to the kitchen now? Does she understand any English?'

'No, hardly a word. I'll come with you. It was a very successful evening and I was proud of you.' Before she could speak he went on, 'Did you like Euphemia? Tane and I have known each other for years, went through medical school together. He almost married a terrible beanpole of a girl he didn't love; Euphemia came along just in time— they're very happy.'

'Yes.' Her throat was suddenly tight with tears. It wasn't that she grudged Euphemia her happiness, only it must be wonderful. . . She went ahead of him, through the green baize door leading to the kitchen and then had to pause because she found herself in a little tiled passage with doors on either side and no kitchen in sight.

'Still rooms and dairy and butler's pantry,' said

Julius behind her, 'the kitchen's straight ahead.'

He stretched past her and opened the door, revealing a room which at first glance appeared to be still in the turn of the century. She had always thought that her mother's kitchen was old fashioned but this one went one further with it's enormous scrubbed table, Aga stove, with chairs on either side of it and a cat asleep on the rug before it. There were vast dressers on either side, bearing row after row of plates and dishes and on the wall a regiment of copper saucepans and polished dish covers. And *Mevrouw* Borren looked exactly right there in her print dress and voluminous apron. There were doors in the farther wall and rooms beyond, Josephine could hear cheerful voices and the sound of dishes being washed.

And yet, as she took a closer look, she could see that there were up-to-date gadgets galore, tucked away discreetly where they wouldn't spoil the old fashioned cosiness of the kitchen. She walked towards the table and was glad when Julius put an arm round her shoulders and spoke to *Mevrouw* Borren, for she had no idea what to say.

The conversation was brief but obviously pleased that lady, for she smiled and bowed her head and then nodded and laughed like a pleased child.

'I told her that you wished to thank her and she says that she enjoyed it all very much and hopes with you here that there will now be many more parties.'

So Josephine, very conscious of his arm, smiled and nodded in her turn and followed Julius through one of the doors to the big tiled room beyond where it seemed that the washing up was done, and here he repeated his short speech to Else and Anna and the middle aged woman who had been in the hall to greet them when they had arrived— *Mevrouw* Tout from the village.

They went back to the drawing room presently where Borren had already removed all traces of the party, coffee cups and glasses had been taken away and the cushions pumped up and the fire set blazing. As they went in he said in his rather peculiar English. 'I bring coffee at once, *Mevrouw*,' and he went briskly through the baize door.

'They'll never get to bed,' observed Josephine.

'They're loving every minute of it. I lived very quietly, my dear, and they had so little to do that they were probably bored to tears. They're positively gleeful at the idea of a little social life.'

Josephine sat down near the fire. 'Didn't you have any social life when you were engaged to. . . When you were engaged?

'Magda preferred to have her parties in restaurants; she found this house gloomy. . .'

'Gloomy? How could she? It's a lovely house and everyone in it is so happy—Borren and his wife and the others and Charlie.' She glanced down at the dog, who had taken up his usual position on his master's feet.

'And you, I hope?' Something in his voice made her look at him, but his face was smilingly bland; she must have imagined. . .wishful thinking, she told herself.

'Oh, yes. I shall be very happy here; I can't

wait to learn Dutch and explore the village and get to know everyone.'

'I hope that I am high on that list of getting to know everyone, Josephine.'

She bent to tickle Charlie's ears. 'Yes, yes of course.' She sought earnestly for something to say and added weakly, 'It's all a bit strange.'

Borren came in with the coffee and she poured them a cup, glad of something to do; Julius was staring at her so hard that she began to worry that her hair had come loose or she had a spot somewhere. He asked abruptly, 'Are you tired? You would like to go to bed when you've had your coffee?' He looked withdrawn and his voice was cool; perhaps he wanted an hour to himself, even as late as this, her father, she remembered, liked to sit in a quiet house after everyone else had gone to bed, and read his medical journals. . . She said quickly. 'Oh, yes, I should. It was a splendid party, wasn't it? And I do like your family—they've all been so kind. . .'

'They had no reason to be otherwise.' He sounded impatient. It was the kind of remark it was so difficult to answer. She drank her coffee so quickly that she burnt her tongue and put her cup down with a sigh of relief which Julius noted with a faint lift of the eyebrows and a twitching lip. 'Well, I'll go to bed,' she said. She sounded uncertain; not a bit like her usual practical self. And when she got up he got up too, kissed her cheek lightly, wished her a good night and went to open the door for her.

Not a happy end to what had been a very happy evening.

She might have known that he would be gone by the time she got down the next morning. Borren and Charlie escorted her to the small room she had liked, where breakfast had been set ready for her and a bright fire was burning. There was a note on her plate, Julius would be home for tea.

She had wondered as she dressed what she would do with her day but she need not have worried; there was another tour of the house, this time with *Mevrouw* Borren and Borren trailing behind, translating for them both, and then a run in the garden with Charlie. The grounds around the house were extensive with a nice wild bit at the far end. Rather like Stoney Bottom, she thought with sudden homesickness. But it was ridiculous to feel homesick; *Mevrouw* Borren seemed determined to spoil her, cooking her a delicious lunch while Borren made sure that she ate it. And in the afternoon since it was dark, and dismal outside, she curled up in the little sitting room with a selection of books and presently dozed off.

When she woke, Julius was sitting in the chair opposite her, reading the paper. When she sat up he lowered it and smiled across at her. 'It's not been too dull?' he wanted to know. 'Borren tells me that you went out with Charlie before lunch. I have to go back to Leiden this evening but I'm free tomorrow morning, we'll go to the village and visit the dominee.'

Josephine sat up straight. 'Oh, good. I'm sorry I was asleep when you got home. I had a lovely morning, going round the house again and taking Charlie round the grounds. You've a lot of land.'

'The grounds? Yes. The fields around belong to the house, of course, and quite a bit of the village.' He studied her face. 'When you're quite used to us, I'll explain it all to you.'

'I only know one side of you,' said Josephine uncertainly. 'I mean when you were at St Michael's you were a surgeon and even at home I don't think I gave much thought to the other sides of you.'

He said lightly, 'Why should you? Time enough for you to get to know me.'

It was like spending an evening with an old friend; easy talk and companionable silences; tea round the fire and later dinner, sitting together at the big table. But it didn't last, of course Julius went away soon after eight o'clock, warning her not to wait up for him.

So she went to bed as soon as she decently could, and lay wakeful until after midnight when she heard the car returning. This was to be her life but she had known that, doctor's wives had to accept that and she was quite prepared to do so, only it would be a lot easier, she thought wistfully, if they were in love, then she could wait up for him as a matter of course, get him a drink when he came in, see that he took a coat with him if it were cold, and make sure that he had his meals. Slow tears trickled down her cheeks and she wiped them away fiercely. She was behaving like an idiot and she wasn't that, she was a sensible young woman who had run a ward very well indeed for several years and was used to dealing with all kinds of people. Only she wasn't sure how to deal with Julius.

With daylight, common sense returned. Time enough to fret and fume when they had been married six months or more! She went down to breakfast, ate a hearty meal in his company, enquired intelligently about the list he had in the afternoon, and set off with him suitably dressed in a tweed skirt and sweater and the sheepskin jacket her father had given her for a wedding present. She had tied a bright scarf over her hair and her face glowed with anticipated pleasure.

They visited the dominee first, a very thin man with a stern face, who offered them coffee while he delivered a severe little lecture about the responsibilities of marriage. His English was good and he used a great many long words, contriving to make the state of matrimony a rather dull business. They bade him a polite goodbye presently and crossed the village square to the local shop. 'Is he a friend of yours?' she asked Julius.

'Oh, hardly that,' he smiled down at her, 'we don't see eye to eye about a number of things—I find his opinion of marriage rather on the stern side, don't you? But we sit on various committees together, and I've no doubt that you will find yourself presiding over various female gatherings. And church, of course, every Sunday—and a long sermon.'

Josephine pulled a face. 'But it'll be good for my Dutch, won't it?'

'Indeed it will. Once Christmas and New Year

are over, the village are getting up some sort of reception for us, but by then you will know a few words of Dutch.'

The village shop was choked with customers. They made way politely for Josephine and Julius and began a round of hand shaking. They each spoke in turn to her and Julius said softly, 'Don't worry, they're telling you their names.'

She smiled endlessly and stood quietly while several of them said a few words, and Julius answered them briefly. She had no idea what he said but they laughed uproariously and shook hands all over again as they left.

'Well, that's the ice broken; they've had a good look at you. In a few days you will get people calling from the neighbourhood and invitations for drinks and dinner. Now we must go to the school; *Juffrouw* Smit will be dying to meet you; besides we have to arrange the time for the children's party. I go every year if I possibly can, just for an hour. We'll go together.'

Juffrouw Smit was a large elderly lady with a rather loud voice and a presence and there was an assistant too, a small, mouselike creature who twittered. There were only three classes and about thirty children in all, most of them from the outlying farms. They stared at Josephine who grinned back at them and waved. One or two of the bolder ones waved back.

They were to attend the party on the next day at two o'clock; Julius and *Juffrouw* Smit made their final arrangements and they all shook hands once more and the children chorused politely.

'Would you like to see the church before we go back?' Julius had taken her arm as they went back towards the square.

'Yes I would. There's time? Borren said lunch would be at twelve. . .'

'Plenty of time, I've. . .' He stopped speaking as a Mercedes sports car came slowly towards them, stopped, and a girl put her head out of the car window and waved.

Josephine, listening to her laughing, excited voice, wished with all her heart that she could understand even one word in ten. And to make matters worse, Julius answered her in his own language before explaining: 'Here is Magda to surprise us, my dear.' It was difficult to tell if he was pleased or not from the blandness of his voice but he showed no sign of discomfort when Magda got out of the car, flung her arms round his neck and kissed him. He introduced them then, observing that probably Magda had heard of his marriage.

Of course, darling!' Her English was fluent and Josephine fumed. 'I just had to see your bride for myself'. She switched her smile to Josephine who smiled just as sweetly back. 'And I'm so glad to meet you, too.' She said with a commendable appearance of pleasure. 'Julius told me about you, of course.'

Magda gave a tinkle of laughter. 'He did? And you risked marrying him?' She turned to Julius. 'And I—I am not married, darling. Oh, I suppose I shall marry Frans but first I wanted to see you again.'

'Well, now you have, and Josephine too. We

are a contented and happy couple.'

'Then you may invite me to lunch and I will judge for myself.' Magda spoke in a joking manner and gave Josephine a malicious glance.

'Yes, do,' said Josephine. 'It has to be early because Julius has to go to Leiden. We were on our way back, if you like to drive ahead. . .'

Her calm grey eyes smiled into wary blue ones. Magda started the engine. 'I'd love to. I'll see you in a few minutes.'

'And why did you do that?' asked Julius as they started to go back from the village. She glanced at his face, there was no sign of annoyance on it, only interest. She said uncertainly, 'I'm not sure. But you're pleased, aren't you?' She gave a sniff. 'After all you were going to marry her.'

'So I was,' agreed Julius silkily.

Borren didn't approve: Josephine was given a reproachful look as they encountered each other in the hall and she said contritely: 'Oh, Borren, has it made it difficult for *Mevrouw* Borren? I'm sorry, I didn't think.'

'There is no difficulty, *Mevrouw*. I did not expect to see *Juffrouw* van Tine again.'

Josephine longed to tell him that she hadn't expected to see her either. 'She'll be going after lunch,' she said comfortingly.

And Magda did: she left at the same time as Julius, telling him delightedly that she would drive behind him to Leiden. 'We'll have time for a little chat if we go now,' she had pointed out.

'That will be nice for you both,' agreed Josephine in a tight voice. 'I expect there's somewhere in the hospital where you can talk.'

She had a certain satisfaction from the thunderous look Julius gave her.

'Back for dinner?' she asked him, briskly cheerful.

'Unless something turns up, my dear.' His polite voice was worse than the frown.

'Don't count on it,' said Magda gaily, 'I've still got a few tricks up my sleeve.'

Josephine watched the Bentley nose its way out of the gates with the Mercedes right behind it. She bubbled with rage and the fear that she had made Julius so angry that he would never forgive her. She fetched a coat, called Charlie and went out of the house, to walk miles along the narrow brick roads, not noticing where she went and not caring either. When she got back it was to find Borren waiting for her, looking worried.

'It is not good that you go out alone, *Mevrouw*,' he told her firmly. 'You do not know where you are, also you may catch a cold.'

'I should have told you I was going for a walk, Borren. I'm quite used to the country, you know, and being by myself, and I had Charlie.'

'*Mijnheer* would not like it, *Mevrouw*.'

She said, 'No, Borren,' meekly, and he took her coat and told her that he would bring her tea to the little sitting room. 'And *Mijnheer* will be home presently,' he told her.

But Julius didn't come home; she had finished her tea and was sitting by the fire doing nothing; when she was called to the 'phone.

'I'll not be home for some hours,' Julius told

her and his voice sounded cool in her ear.

'I thought perhaps you wouldn't be.' She was ashamed of her waspish voice as she spoke, but that didn't stop her slamming the receiver back.

She dined alone at the big table in the dining room, looked after by a silently sympathetic Borren and for some reason best known to herself she had elected to change into one of her prettiest dresses. She swallowed down the delicious food put before her, replied suitably to the old man's fatherly urging to have second helpings and then went to the drawing-room for her coffee, where she sat with Charlie for company, getting crosser and crosser with every minute; in fact rage had far outstripped for the moment at least, the fear that Julius had fallen in love with the wretched Magda all over again and if so, what on earth was she to do? She went over this problem for a long time until her head ached and then sat wondering what he was doing. Dining somewhere discreet with the horrid woman, she had no doubt, she told herself furiously, and she could hardly blame him; Magda was quite beautiful and full of little feminine tricks which try as she would Josephine had never been much good at.

When the great *stoel* clock on the wall chimed a silvery eleven, she got a coat from the cloakroom and went into the garden with Charlie. It was bitterly cold but she didn't notice that, only when she got back indoors and went to warm her numbed fingers by the fire she realised that she was shivering. 'I shall die of pneumonia,' said

Josephine with morbid satisfaction, 'and he'll be full of remorse.'

Charlie nudged her gently away from the hearth and settled himself in the warmth, and she wished him good night, bade Borren good night too as she went through the hall and upstairs. The corridor leading to her room was softly lighted and the glow shone on the old paintings on the walls and the gleaming parquet floor. Already in a very bad temper, the atmosphere of the old house fired her imagination. 'I shall haunt him,' she said in a whisper, 'I'll wear the white nightie with ruffles. . .'

She took a long time getting ready for bed and there was still no sign of Julius returning. She heard Borren locking up and then silence. Too put out to sleep, she got out of bed, put on the pink quilted dressing gown and the little slippers Mike and Natalie had given her, and went silently downstairs. There was a wall light on in the hall and the door to the drawing room had been left open; she could see Charlie stretched out before the still brightly burning fire. He had his basket in the kitchen at night but as Borren had been at pains to tell her, when his Master was out at night, Charlie was allowed to wait for him. 'So I'll wait too,' declared Josephine.

She curled up in one of the chairs drawn up to the fire and presently, lulled by the warmth and Charlie's whispered snores, dozed off. She wakened when Julius opened the house door and by the time he entered the drawing-room she was sitting up very straight, wide awake, a returning tide of rage washing over her.

Julius had stopped in the doorway. 'My dear Josephine, why are you not in bed?'

The blandness of his voice was all she needed. 'And about time too,' she said a shade too loudly, ignoring his question. 'I suppose you've spent the evening with Magda and she's been telling you what an awful mistake you made getting married to me. Well I daresay you're right. . .'

Julius had come to sit on the chair at the other side of the hearth. He appeared totally unsurprised at her outburst, indeed, he looked amused.

'You're very cross,' was all he said. 'Are you jealous?'

'Pooh,' said Josephine and tossed her bright hair over her shoulders, quite unaware of how delightful she looked. 'Why should I be jealous?'

'I can think of several reasons.' He smiled and she saw then that he was very tired.

She said 'Pooh,' again and got up. 'I'm going to bed. You look tired and I'm not surprised. Magda must keep a man on his toes.'

She swept to the door, rather spoiling the effect by tripping over her dressing gown, only to find him there too.

'You are a very silly girl,' he told her quietly, 'as blind as a bat, and your head so stuffed with nonsense that you can't think straight. We'll talk in the morning.'

If she had answered him she would have burst into tears; she went up to her room, closed the door and flung herself on the bed to have a good cry.

She couldn't cry for ever; presently she got into

bed and curled up in a ball in its luxurious warmth and went over the events of the last half hour. She had been silly to have lost her temper, he had married her because she was so suitable as a companion, calm and serene and not easily put out, and she had raged at him like a fishwife. 'Not that he didn't deserve every word,' she mumbled into the bedclothes, all the same she quite saw that in the morning she would have to apologise, and if he had discovered that he loved Magda after all, then she would have to step aside with what grace she could muster. Perhaps, she thought miserably, he had felt sure that Magda didn't matter to him any more; that it was safe for him to marry and settle down to an ordered life, only Magda had turned up again and charmed the heart from him. It wasn't anyone's fault, just fate, though fate had been given a good shove from the beastly Magda. Josephine closed her eyes; she would have to get some sleep; she dropped off presently trying to calculate how quickly a marriage could be annulled.

Her face was a mess in the morning; she did the best she could with it, put on a thick sweater and skirt and went downstairs, preserving a calm she didn't feel.

There was no one in the dining room but as she went in Borren pottered in behind her to tell her that *Mijnheer* had left early for the hospital and had breakfasted an hour since. If he found it strange that she didn't know that already he forebore from commenting, and a glance at her puffy eyelids and pink nose sent him fussing around her, bringing hot coffee and croissants, boiled eggs and cheese, and kept him there, making sure that she ate something. Only when she had had her coffee and eaten a croissant did he hand her a note from Julius. It was brief and businesslike, merely stating that as he would probably be away from home all day, would she go to the village school, make his excuses to *Juffrouw* Smit and stay for half an hour at the children's party?

She would have to go; indeed, it never entered her head not to. It would be unthinkable to break the yearly tradition just because she and Julius weren't on speaking terms. She confided in Borren and asked him if there was anything special she should do.

'*Mijnheer* always takes a large tin of sweets with him; of course when *Mevrouw* van Tacx was alive she went, always dressed very smartly, because of course the children liked that.'

'Well, I'll do the same. It's at two o'clock, isn't it? Do I walk to the village, Borren?'

He looked shocked. 'Oh, no, *Mevrouw*. I shall drive you. If it suits you lunch will be at twelve o'clock and then there will be ample time.'

She thanked him, finished her breakfast, whistled to a delighted Charlie and went for a walk, wrapped warmly in the sheepskin jacket. The day was gloomy, just as she was gloomy, which seemed all wrong with Christmas only a stone's throw away—she had never felt less festive. Perhaps if Julius would agree, she could go home for a few days? She would cool off and they could talk sensibly. It struck her that he had talked

sensibly anyway; it was she who had shouted and
lost her temper. Something she so very seldom
did. She didn't really want to go home; how could
she bear to leave him, even if he ignored her, or
worse, treated her with that awful bland politeness.
Just like one of his ward rounds, only now she
couldn't take refuge behind her uniform.

She obediently ate the lunch laid before her and
went to her room to go through her wardrobe and
find something suitable. The fur coat and hat, of
course, and the pearls and a misty green crêpe
dress with a wide collar and a big satin bow under
her chin. High heeled shoes since she wouldn't
have to walk, and matching handbag and gloves.
Dressed, she took a long look at her reflection.
She looked the very picture of a landed
gentleman's wife.

Borren, in a thick coat and a peaked cap, was
waiting for her in the hall, a large tin of sweets
under his arm. 'Will I do, Borren?' she asked
worriedly and was rewarded by his: 'Oh, yes,
Mevrouw. If you would step into the kitchen and
show *Mevrouw* Borren and the girls?'

Their pleased admiration did her cold heart
good. At least Julius wouldn't have been ashamed
of her. She got into a dark blue Jaguar she hadn't
seen outside the door, obeying Borren's 'The back
seat if *Mevrouw* will allow,' and was driven in
some state the short distance to the schoolhouse.

She was hollow with fright as she got out of
the car, threw Borren a speaking glance, and shook
hands with *Juffrouw* Smit and her assistant. The
children were crowded into the largest classroom,

silent except for the odd sniff and shuffle. They stared at her until *Juffrouw* Smit said in a commanding voice, '*Kinderen*,' when they obediently chorused, '*Dag, Mevrouw van Tacx*.'

Josephine shifted the tin of sweets and smiled widely. 'Hullo,' she said and walked farther into the room. The children melted away slowly and then just as slowly pressed close to her. She took off her coat and gave it to a boy standing near, and gave her gloves and handbag to a little girl beside him. The sweets she dumped on a nearby window sill.

'What do we do first?' She asked *Juffrouw* Smit.

'There are games, *Mevrouw*. If you care to sit and watch. . .'

'Oh, I'll join in—I like games,' said Josephine cheerfully. 'Shall we start?'

The party was a little slow to get off the ground, the children were shy and very much on their best behaviour, but Josephine, seeing a box of balloons waiting to be blown up, led the way, soon they were all puffing and blowing and shrieking and presently batting them to and fro across the room, making a good deal of noise. Josephine, catching sight of *Juffrouw* Smit's severe face, wondered if she should have sat on a chair after all and done nothing, but the children, their shyness forgotten, were enjoying them around and while they were munching, looked around, seeking inspiration. She found it at once, a tape recorder on top of the old fashioned upright piano, and *Juffrouw* Smit came across the room to say, 'One of the children brought it here; his father owns it, he thought it would be nice. . .'

'Oh, rather,' said Josephine, already poking around the few tapes beside it. 'Let's have it on, we can dance the conga.' She beamed at her companion who blinked and said, 'Just as *Mevrouw* wishes.' Josephine found that rather daunting, but once she had got the tape started, something loud and monotonous from the top twenty, she asked *Juffrouw* Smit to tell the children to line up behind her and no time at all they were off, snaking around the room, shouting and laughing, and on the second time round Josephine seized *Juffrouw* Smit and her little assistant and pushed them in between the children.

The noise was fearful; Julius, pausing to take off his coat in the little porch, stood and watched his wife capering at the head of the children, she looked quite beautiful, enjoying herself with the unselfconsciousness of a child. He took his eyes off her just long enough to take in the interesting spectacle of the school teachers capering along at the end of the snake. The assistant was enjoying herself, *Juffrouw* Smit wore the resigned look of someone who has just discovered that nothing will ever be the same again.

The snake turned and Josephine saw him and came slowly to a halt not more than a yard or so from him. The children crowded round, jumping up and down, wanting to go on, but knowing that *Mijnheer* van Tacx, kind though he was, wasn't likely to join in.

Josephine had forgotten the children, she was

staring at Julius her heart racing, for he was looking at her in a way which had turned the drab
schoolroom into a heaven. She said in a squeaky
voice, 'Julius?'

'My dear, I got away earlier than I had expected.
I see that you are making a great success of the
party.' He came and took her hand and kissed her
cheek and then shook hands with the two school-
teachers.

'Time for the feast?' he enquired and waved to
the children, who waved back.

It was obvious to Josephine that in the village
at least, his word was a kindly law. The children
were herded on to long forms around trestle tables
and invited to fall to. And with an air of someone
who had done it all a great many times, Julius
produced a bottle of champagne, opened it, filled
four glasses and toasted the teachers. And after
that for a short time it was bustling to and fro
around the tables, and making sure that the children were getting what they wanted. The food,
Josephine observed, was abundant and just what
children craved; potato crisps, sandwiches, saus-
ages on sticks, *speculaas*, a traditional biscuit
studded with almonds. She had no doubt that Julius
had provided the lot. The quantities of fizzy lem-
onade which was consumed made her shudder.

Presently she found herself standing beside
Julius, watching the children and Miss Smit,
rendered positively girlish by reason of the
champagne and the large be-ribboned package
Julius had given her. Even the little assistant
had stopped twittering while she turned a similar

package over and over, longing to open it, but not wishing to do so until *Juffrouw* Smit had opened her own. It was quieter now, only a steady munching could be heard. In a little while now the children would go home, each clutching the envelope Julius had handed to each one; another time honoured custom, thought Josephine, a traditional Christmas Box.

'Time we were going,' said Julius, quietly. 'A most successful afternoon I fancy: the village will love you.'

'Don't we stay to the end?' asked Josephine who didn't want to but had a sudden shyness about being alone with him.

'No, We will go home and have that little talk. . .and this time I'll get it right.'

She turned her head to look at him, his eyes were very bright and very blue and he was smiling. 'Get what right?' she asked.

'The time and the place.' He picked up her coat and she put it on, shook hands with the teachers, waved goodbye to the children and went with him to the Bentley outside. He was silent during the short drive back to the house, and she, feverishly turning over suitable small talk in her head, was frightfully glad when they got there.

The house welcomed them, lights glowing against the darkening day outside, a great fire burning in the drawing room and Borren appearing in a stately fashion to close the door after them and hope that the afternoon had been a success.

'Remarkably so,' Julius told him. '*Mevrouw* was splendid, I can see that she is going to a great asset to the village. . .she likes children.'

He glanced at her as she spoke and quite without knowing why she blushed.

'I'll just go upstairs,' she began, anxious to get away and calm down.

'Presently, my dear.' Julius was at his most bland. He put a large compelling arm round her shoulders and guided her towards the drawing room.

'Borren, may we have tea in half an hour please? And I don't want to be disturbed. Take any calls will you? and unless they are really urgent save them.'

He went unhurriedly into the drawing room, taking Josephine with him and shutting the door firmly behind them. He released her then and leaned against the door watching her.

'At last—the time and the place, but only you can tell me if I have the loved one, Josephine, my darling.'

Her heart soared but she wouldn't look at him. Instead she said soberly? 'And Magda? Is she your darling too?' At the thought of the girl she very nearly ground her teeth.

'No—and never has been'. He spoke very quietly.

'You went off together,' stated Josephine, not quite accurately.'

'So we did—in separate cars and I haven't seen her since.'

'Then why didn't you come home. . .?' To her shame Josephine choked on a sob.

'There was a perforation—a woman with a

large family and a loving husband—well worth trying to save.' He paused. 'Josephine, I fell in love with you the very first time I saw you, I wanted you for my wife but you were afraid of being hurt again, weren't you? So I persuaded you to marry me because I knew that sooner or later you would come to love me too.'

He hadn't moved from the door. 'A silly girl and as blind as a bat,' he said softly, 'and I love her to distraction.'

Josephine had had her back to him. Now she turned round slowly. 'I didn't know—not at first, and then I thought. . .then Magda came.'

A jumble of words so unlike her usual way of talking that Julius smiled. He said, 'You make it very clear, my dear love.' He left the door at last and took her in his arms. They felt strong and comforting around her and she laid her head with a little sigh against his chest. But she wasn't allowed to leave it there; he put a hand under her chin and turned her face up to his and began to kiss her.

It was some time later when she pulled away from him just a little.

Julius—dear Julius. We ought to sit down and talk. . .'

'Why my darling? I'm very happy as I am and I thought that you were too.'

'Oh, I am'. She kissed him to prove her words. 'But there's such a lot. . . Christmas, and Euphemia wants us to go to dinner, and Borren said something about a Christmas Tree.'

'All pleasant topics of conversation and none

of them urgent.' He bent his head to hers. 'But this is'.

There was, Josephine considered in a dreamy fashion, no point in arguing with him.